**He leaned close
until her back w
placed one hand on the wall by her head
and half caged her with his body.**

"You look delicious."

She made a dismissive noise. Knowing she wanted to
test the kitchen, she'd thrown on a V-neck T-shirt and
put her hair in a ponytail. "I look like a farmhand."

His eyes dipped into the V of her shirt, making her
breathing increase slightly. He hadn't even touched her,
yet her body was screaming for him. His knowing gaze
came up to hers.

"What would you do if I kissed you right now?"

"I'd leave."

He frowned. "Really? I don't think so."

"I thought we were going to cultivate our working
relationship."

"We are." His lips moved closer and their breaths
mingled.

"I thought we were going to forget what happened."

His fingertip ran down her arm. "Can you forget,
angel? Because I'm having a hard time."

She shivered, not sure when the name had gone from
an annoyance to an endearment she craved hearing.

Dear Reader,

I hope you are ready to get swept away in gourmet dishes and sweet sips of wine. *A Taste of Pleasure* was a chance for me to indulge in a bit of Italian luxury. During my time in Italy, I was captivated by the food, the wine…and the men, which was why it was so easy to imagine a hero as sexy as Antonio Lorenzetti. With a divorce behind him and his family in trouble, the successful restaurateur gets help from an unexpected place.

When chef Danica Nilsson loses her boyfriend and her restaurant, her world falls apart, but Toni holds the key to a new opportunity and eventually her heart. Writing Toni and Dani was so much fun. This book is ultimately a romance, but it's also about broken dreams, and how love and support is a gourmet recipe that can heal all.

Happy reading!

Chloe Blake

A TASTE OF
Pleasure
Chloe Blake

HARLEQUIN® KIMANI™ ROMANCE

Recycling programs
for this product may
not exist in your area.

ISBN-13: 978-1-335-21677-9

A Taste of Pleasure

HARLEQUIN®

Printed in U.S.A.

TM www.Harlequin.com

Chloe Blake can be found dreaming up stories while she is traveling the world or just sitting on her couch in Brooklyn, New York. When she is not writing sexy novels, she is at the newest wine bar, taking random online classes, binge-watching Netflix or searching for her next adventure. Readers can find out more about Chloe and her books from her website at www.chloeblakebooks.com.

Books by Chloe Blake

Harlequin Kimani Romance

A Taste of Desire
A Taste of Pleasure

To Amy, who found a happily-ever-after of her own.

Acknowledgments

My heartfelt thanks to my agent, Christine Witthohn,
and to the team at Harlequin Kimani Romance.
My love and appreciation goes to my friends,
who are my chosen family. And last, my biggest thanks
to the readers who chose this book.
Your support inspires me to keep writing.

Chapter 1

Chef Danica Nilsson spread her knives on the long table and plucked the twelve-inch slicer from its pocket. With the bride and groom's cake cutting ritual finished, it was time to serve the flowered and jeweled creation she had baked to the three hundred wedding guests that flew to Brazil to see her best friend Nicole get married.

"He's looking at you again." Liz, a longtime friend to her and the bride, leaned on the tabletop and crossed her arms.

Dani didn't look up as she worked. "Maybe he's crazy."

"Crazy doesn't look *that* good. That man is handsome."

Dani half listened as she urged herself to hurry. The seven-layer masterpiece had been chilled to withstand the Brazilian heat, but even sitting under the shade of the tent, which had been spread across the entire vineyard, the icing was beginning to sheen.

"Maybe he wants some cake."

"Oh, he definitely wants some *cake*." Liz raised her brows and stared at Dani's ass. Dani shook her head at her friend, thinking that she had enough "cake" to feed all of Brazil.

"Wasn't he married to a model or something? He's not trying for—" Dani looked down at her size-sixteen figure "—all of this."

"You never know. Sometimes people go for the complete opposite of what they've had before." Dani heard Liz take her therapy tone, something the good doctor did unconsciously when she was trying to make a point.

"I'm not trying to find a man here, Liz."

"I just want you to have a little fun…and to forget about Andre."

With just the sound of his name, Dani felt her guard go up. She'd *been* trying to forget, but the more she tried, the more she thought about him. Andre had refused to attend the wedding with her and had made it clear he didn't harbor the same feelings for her that she had for him.

Andre loved running the New York restaurant together—translation: he loved that she did all the work running the kitchen, but anything more than sex was out of the question.

Dani picked up her knife and squeezed.

"Look, you go for him. I'm gonna cut this cake."

The guests drank and danced as Dani took apart the layers and began plating slices of each. At first each cut made her feel more single, but as she worked she began to feel better.

The cake was her gift to the couple, a chef's gift, and each layer was infused with different ingredients that told the story of their love—the bold New Yorker and the brooding Frenchman finding each other on a vineyard in Brazil.

A Brazilian chocolate sponge foundation, Nicole's favorite, with a second layer of lavender French vanilla, Destin's favorite. A third layer of traditional Brazilian fruitcake and a fourth layer of New York cheesecake. The last three layers she was most proud of, a Cab Franc–infused red velvet. All topped with wine-infused icing and candy jewels.

"*Dio mio*…is that wine? *Brava!* You're an artist," said a deep accented voice. Dani pulled her focus from slicing the cake to find Antonio Dante Lorenzetti, Destin's best man, licking his finger.

"Did you just stick your finger in my cake?" The grip on her knife tightened.

Toni licked his lips and flashed a boyish smile. Sweat darkened his honey-colored hair around the temples, and his shirt was open to reveal a slightly damp chest. She briefly craned her neck to take in all six feet and three inches of him.

Liz was right, he *was* handsome. He was the type of guy that could have any girl he wanted. She wondered which one he'd choose to take back to his room.

Shit! Her cut faltered, breaking one of the perfectly two-inch cake slices in half.

"Sorry." Toni shrugged an apology and slipped his hands in his pockets. His sleeves were rolled and a glint was in his eye, making him look undeniably masculine.

Dani set the knife down and rose to her full five-foot-eight-inch height. She quickly dabbed at the sweat on her brow with a towel. And if Toni hadn't been standing there, she would have dabbed at her cleavage, as well. The brides-maid dress her friend chose hugged her full frame nicely, but the open neckline showed a bit too much cleavage for Dani's taste.

"Nice ink." His gaze ran over the colorful swirls of flowers and symbols on the tan skin of her left forearm. Dani studied his expression; some people had a thing against tattoos, but Dani saw no signs of aversion. Still, she was certain that a woman like her was definitely not what he was used to.

Dani pulled her shoulder-length hair into a bun on her head, the shaved undercut of her hairstyle letting in more cool air. Screw decorum, she wiped at her cleavage, then tossed the towel on the table. She lifted a brow when she caught his gaze rising from her breasts. *Men.*

"What can I do for you, Toni?"

"You looked like you needed help."

"A finger in my food is not help."

He smirked. "I mean, where is the champagne for the dessert?" She looked around. Good question.

"I thought Anton was rounding it up with the catering staff."

Toni frowned and leaned closer, swiping his pointer finger through the icing of the broken cake by Dani's side.

"You're lucky I don't cut that finger off."

"*Bella*, you won't serve that piece." His lips attacked said finger. "The icing is subtle, to complement the sweetness of the cake I assume? Lovely. You need the Clos d'Ambonnay for this."

"No, I asked for the Lambrusco."

"Absolutely not. That will be too sweet."

Dani fought the urge to stab him.

His Italian arrogance aside, she remembered Destin introducing Toni to her as a fine wine merchant, and currently working to distribute Deschamps, Destin and Nicole's award-winning wines. His family had been restaurateurs in Italy for generations. Apparently, he knew wine and food.

But so did Dani. She'd been cooking with one of Milan's premier chef's since she was a teenager, but she wasn't going to throw her experience, her schooling in France or her current two-star Michelin restaurant in New York in his face.

What she was going to do was try to respect the groom by not killing his friend.

"Look, Toni, we've already had our tastings and this is the wine Nicole prefers with the cake. You know how sensitive her palate is. So thank you for the suggestion but I've got it under control. And I don't think we ordered any Clos so—"

"I brought some with me. Just in case you ran out. Six cases of Lambrusco seemed low to me, but then again Italians are prone to excess."

Dani's hands flew to her hips.

"And how would you know how much I ordered?"

Toni rocked on his heels. "You ordered it from me."

Dani blinked. "We ordered from a Brazilian warehouse."

"My warehouse."

Dani looked him up and down. No wonder he was so arrogant; he didn't work for the distributor, he owned it.

He smiled. "Don't worry, I gave them a discount."

Yep. Money was no object. She should have known by that close-cut beard, which was perfectly trimmed to look like five o'clock shadow.

The catering staff appeared with wine bottles and began filling the idle flutes with bubbly—some red, the Lambrusco, and some mysterious white, which Dani assumed was the Clos. Dani slid her gaze to Toni, who was averting his eyes toward the guests.

"Well, looks like someone found your Clos."

Toni's apologetic smile was the perfect match of sheepish and wicked.

The staff took the plated desserts to the tables and left fresh dishes for her use. Dani bit her tongue and took up her knife again, unwilling to tell him that having red and white bubbly for the dessert was a good idea.

Ignoring him, she grabbed another layer of cake and prepped it for cutting.

"What restaurant did you say you worked in again?"

"Via L'Italy," she said over her shoulder, surprised he was still standing there. Her knife made quick work of the cake.

"The one on Bond street? Isn't that Andre Pierre's restaurant?"

Dani's knife faulted again and a fruit-filled slice crumbled.

Biting her cheek, she slowly lowered the knife to the table and faced him.

"It's *my* kitchen."

He frowned. "So are you a sous-chef?"

"I'm *head* chef."

His frown got deeper. "Alongside Andre?"

Yeah, it sounded ridiculous. Dani took a deep breath, unable to bring herself to say the term *ghost chef.* But that's what she was. She was the blood sweat and tears behind Andre, the famous chef who conceptualized the restaurant. A YouTube phenomenon turned celebrity chef, Andre opened several restaurants in the world under his name, but never stepped one foot inside the kitchens.

She had taken the job years ago thinking she would be working directly with a master. She found out quickly that he was limited in his skills. Proper editing and a ghost chef equaled smoke and mirrors. Many times she'd thought of leaving, but once the restaurant began earning Michelin stars, Andre made it worth her while to stay.

They had even begun sleeping together.

The kitchen was hers, the menu was hers and the Michelin stars…they were because of her.

But to the outside world, it was all Andre.

Dani let her gaze fall, unable to meet his bright blue questioning look. She arranged the broken slice on a small plate with a fork and handed it to him.

"Yes, Andre and I collaborate quite well."

Toni took a bite and uttered a low groan of pleasure. She hated that his reaction made her proud…and a little aroused.

They'd been at the same table for dinner. He ate like a bear, dipping into everything, taking his time with the dishes he liked, eating seconds and sometimes thirds. She'd always liked a healthy appetite in a man.

Not that she was watching, or wondering if he made love the same way.

He slid the fork from his lips.

"That cake is art. Maybe you'll cook for me one day?"

Her eyes snapped to his clear gaze. Was he flirting?

"I mean, I could come to your restaurant."

Of course, he wasn't attracted to her. He liked super-thin arm candy that ate salads and wore tons of makeup. She pressed her lips together. Her lipstick had melted off hours ago.

"Sure. Stop by next time you're in New York," she said politely.

"Erm…you have—" He stepped closer and reached for her.

"What?" She looked down her body.

He swiped a finger across her upper breast and a jolt tore through her. Shocked, she followed his hand, which pulled away with a small dollop of icing on his finger.

She grabbed a towel and handed it to him, but he shook his head and placed the tip of his finger in his mouth.

"So good. I get another piece at the table, yes?"

She nodded absently as he walked away, blinking against the tingly sensations that lingered on her skin and swirled through her body.

Toni stood at the edge of the crowd and watched the throng of women in evening wear get ready to fight over the bouquet. The bride teased the group with a wave of her flowers, then turned her back.

Toni sighed and smoothed a hand over his brow.

I can't do this anymore, Toni. I don't want this life.

He downed the rest of his champagne and turned to go. He couldn't watch anymore.

A large hand landed on his shoulder. "She's hot for you, man. She's been staring at you all night."

Toni forced himself back around and smirked along with his fellow groomsman. Reluctantly he slid his gaze to the thin blonde in the red dress and sure enough, she was staring right at him.

She smiled. He forced a grin back in an effort to be polite, but he quickly looked away.

Virgin Mary help him.

She was beautiful…and way too reminiscent of his ex-wife. Being just out of a divorce, weddings were not high on his attendance list, but he couldn't let Destin down. Nor did he want to bring his baggage to the happy day.

Toni turned his head to where the groom was staring lovingly at his bride. Toni supposed he'd done the same at his wedding.

This isn't want I signed up for.

He tried to shake the angry voice of his ex-wife from his head. He lifted his glass to his lips. Empty. When the show was over he'd head to the bar, and then everything would be all right.

Fortified by his new plan he looked up and prayed the spectacle would soon be over. There was a shot of whiskey with his name on it. Toni focused on the bride, who had stopped midthrow and was waving at someone. His thoughts were wiped from his brain.

Danica let her curling hair fall around her shoulders and made her way from the cake station into the crowd of single ladies. He licked his lips, as if trying to taste the icing that had landed on her cleavage again. And what a stunning bosom it was. She was tall and hourglass shaped with full hips that he couldn't take his eyes from as she walked in her heels.

"That's too much woman for you, bro."

Toni chuckled.

"There is no such thing as too much woman, Leo."

Leo laughed in agreement and slapped him on the back.

"You can't have all of 'em. Save some for the rest of us."

"Don't worry, brother. I only want one." He was half kidding, thinking that a good night's sleep didn't sound so bad. But as Dani stood close to the back and slightly away from the women jostling for position, he couldn't help but imagine her naked in his sheets.

The bride tossed the bouquet and he compared the scene before him to the game-winning goal in the World Cup. The girls moved as one toward the airborne flowers. The blonde in the red dress dove. Dani put her arms up for the block. The blonde grazed the bouquet and tipped it into Dani's hands.

The crowd oohed.

But Dani swatted it into the hands of a young flower girl while the blonde lost her footing and hit the ground.

The crowd ahhed.

The blonde looked pissed. Dani sauntered away. And Toni headed for the bar.

Dani put the top layer of the wedding cake in the refrigerator for the newlyweds, closed the door and officially ended her maid of honor duties. Although the DJ was still playing, the party had thinned out once the bride and groom conspicuously disappeared. And it took Dani a minute to realize that her friend Liz had also left with one of the groomsmen, which meant the Dani would have to enjoy one last drink alone.

She found a seat at the bar, ordered a shot of whiskey, and paid no attention to the tall, broad-shouldered man with his back to her. Her thoughts drifted back to her encounter with the best man. Who did he think he was arguing with her over the wine? He looked damn good in a suit though. And those eyes, they glittered like a rainbow after a storm.

Dani cursed her weakness for tall, handsome and cocky.

As for Andre, when she got back to New York, she'd put an end to their sexual relationship.

If she could just find a sweet, humble, not shorter than herself man, then life would be perfect. Okay, maybe he could be a little shorter than her, but he'd have to have muscles to complement her figure.

And he'd have to be cool with her work schedule. Running a kitchen was a 24/7 job, which is why she had a penchant for sleeping with her coworkers. She sighed. This cycle had to stop.

Dani's gaze darted back and forth, and then she pulled out her phone and opened up her dating app. Swipe left, swipe left, swipe left. Someone brushed by her back and she pulled her phone close. No one needed to know how pathetic she had gotten to be swiping at a wedding. When the coast was clear she made one more swipe.

"He's cute," said a deep accented voice behind her.

Mortified, Dani sat up and pulled her phone to her chest, ignoring the goose bumps his voice sent down her bare arms. Slipping her phone back in her purse, she slowly turned and met Toni's amused steady gaze.

His hair was spiked like he'd been running his hand through it, but he still looked gorgeous.

"Stop sneaking up on me."

"Sorry, I didn't mean to interrupt," he said with a smirk. "Aren't there enough eligible men here for you?"

They both turned when one of the more inebriated guests fell off his chair.

She chuckled and turned back to him, her gaze caught in the ripples of his chest as he too laughed.

"Um, No. And I'm not really looking for a guy, I was just having a drink before I went to bed."

"What a coincidence. Me too." He downed his whiskey and held up two fingers. "Bartender, two more."

Dani held up her hands, then gestured toward the empty stool. "No, no, I'm not trying to be that guy." But before she could slip away he leaned in so she could feel his warm breath on her cheek.

"Then how about we find more of that icing, and you can tell me which body parts you want me to lick it off of."

Shock had her turning her head slowly, unsure if she had heard him correctly. His heavy-lidded gaze held hers and an explosion of sexual heat shot to the tips of her breasts, which were now diamond points, down to the V between her thighs, which felt on fire, and down her legs to the tips of her toes.

Time slowed and her heart pounded.

"It's just one night," he whispered, sensing her hesitation. "I'm going back to Milan tomorrow."

"Milan? I didn't know you were from Milan."

"It doesn't matter."

Without breaking eye contact, he brought the back of her hand to his lips and kissed the warm skin, making every cell in her body shiver with unnamed desire. Suddenly nothing mattered but him.

"Let's go," she exhaled, hoping she had enough icing to cover him, as well.

Chapter 2

They left the reception separately with a plan. Dani would grab the icing and meet Toni in his room, which sat ocean side on the ground floor of the resort.

Unfortunately Dani was out of icing, but they still had a case of Clos left and what better way to enjoy a $1700 bottle of champagne then before, during and after sex.

Dani was inside the walk-in pantry when two strong arms appeared by her temples.

"I got impatient."

Toni was at her back, reaching over her to help keep the wine locker open and simultaneously kissing his way down the back of her neck.

"There is no more icing. I'm improvising."

She pulled two bottles from the slats, and then backed into him to shut the door.

"I like how you think. Mmm, you smell like vanilla," he said low against her nape. He was a solid wall of muscle and she shamelessly rubbed her body against him. His hands found their way over her hips and ran up her front to cup her breasts.

She struggled to keep hold of the bottles, feeling exposed to his roaming hands, and tightened her grip. Never would she waste such a beautiful bottle of wine, and never could she walk away from the pleasure this man was offering.

The briefest thought of Andre came and went, replaced by a sense of entitlement. She deserved to feel wanted and she was going to take what Toni was offering.

Toni spun her around and captured her mouth in a kiss so deep, so powerful, that Dani was instantly lost. She almost whimpered when he pulled back and took the bottles of champagne from her grip.

Her chest heaved as she leaned against the wine locker and watched him open one of the bottles with a loud pop. He held the bottle to his lips and exposed the strong column of his throat, and then he brought his mouth to hers.

The sweet wine trickled into her mouth as he nipped at her lips, biting softly at the sensitive flesh. He paused again, holding the opening to her lips. She closed her eyes and drank deeply, swallowing the fizzy elixir, thinking in some way she was taking him inside her.

When she opened her eyes, he was standing over her, his gaze fixed on the front of her dress. She arched her back in a sexy tease, and he groaned.

"*Potrei guardarti tutto il giorno.* You look beautiful in that dress, but it needs to come off."

The pulsing between her legs got stronger at his words. His fingers traced the plunging U-shaped neckline of her dress, softly trailing the quivering flesh of her cleavage. He watched her face as he cupped her breast and ran a thumb over the small dots made by her straining nipples.

She ran a hand over his shoulder to cup the back of his head.

"We aren't going to make it out of here, are we?"

He looked down at the front of his pants. Her mouth went dry at the straining outline of his erection. "I'm not sure I can walk."

"Then do what you want to me, and the dress."

His eyes flashed. Before she knew it, the bottles were discarded and he hiked her skirt up around her waist. Her breath left her body when Toni's fingers ran up the back of her thighs to the naked flesh of her ass. He kneaded her backside with bold strokes, fingering her lacy panties, then pulled one of her legs up, pushing past the wisp of fabric.

Dani arched into his hand, grinding, wordlessly begging. The mound of his palm and his gentle kisses drove her into an insatiable frenzy.

Dani had always been conscious of her body when making love, but the way he was touching her, gazing at her, made her want to tear at her clothing until she was offered up to him naked and raw.

And she wanted him naked too.

She grabbed at his shirt and tore it open, soliciting a wicked smirk from him. Her fingers trailed over the crest-like tattoo on his left pectoral and found their way down his hard torso to cup the huge, hard shaft that was pressing against his tuxedo pants—she swallowed hard.

With her other hand, she forced his face to hers and plunged her tongue into his mouth. A collective moan came from beneath their kiss. He lifted his mouth from hers. "I want to see you," he said in a low voice.

Dani turned around and felt Toni's mouth on her nape as he slowly tugged down her zipper. He then took the opportunity to run his lips up and down her spine, causing her to lose her mind with need.

She slowly turned back around and let the dress slump down her shoulders and catch on the edge of her strapless bra. One small movement and the dress would hit the floor. He reached for the bunched up fabric, but she playfully slapped his hand away. He whimpered and she laughed. She liked teasing him. Liked being in control.

She reached for his open shirt and yanked it off his shoulders.

"I want to taste you," she said, and then her lips and tongue found the strong pulse of his neck. He massaged her back, sending shock waves over her skin. In seconds, her strapless bra was on the floor, and his sure fingers wrenched at her dress, pulling it down over her hips in a flame-hot caress that ended with her lifted into his arms and her legs wrapped around him.

Wine bottles rattled as her back hit the wine locker. Toni widened his legs and wedged their bodies against the glass door. Dani reached for his belt as he brought his mouth to her breasts, licking and sucking at the sides of the soft, plump flesh.

Dani moaned, her hands full of Toni's thick, sandy-colored hair, her head thrown back, her back arched. She pushed herself against him, unapologetic in her pursuit of pleasure, begging for the sweet agony of his onslaught.

"Patience," he teased, taking her ample breasts into his hands. Reverently, he ran his thumbs lightly over the tight buds, then back again.

"*Sei bella.* You're beautiful," he said softly. His mouth found every square inch of her breasts, rising up from her rib cage to the sensitive tips of her nipples.

"Please," she whimpered, her sounds of pleasure mingled with the jingle of the bottles. In answer, he carefully lowered her feet to the ground, and then he kissed his way down her body, taking her panties down her thighs and untangling them from her ankles.

He crumped the lace in his hand, looked into her eyes and brought the fabric to his nose.

"Vanilla and spice," he groaned.

Suddenly, Toni's head was between her legs, his hands on the back of her thighs and his tongue between her folds. "Yes," she gasped, throwing her head back as pleasure so deep and raw sang through her body. She instinctively opened her legs up wider and pressed her hips up into his mouth. He held her firmly, laving her with long, slow strokes. She tangled her fingers into the hair on the top of his head and moved her hips in rhythm with his tongue.

Never had she been so hot for a man. Not even Andre

had made her wild like this. She cupped her breasts and toyed with her nipples, enhancing what he was doing to her, unconcerned if someone discovered them.

"You taste better than the icing," he said before he reached for her and brought her mouth to his. She tasted herself on his lips and felt her insides go liquid.

"Please, Toni," she begged, her legs parting wider, her body searching for his. He ran his hands over her thighs and leaned just inches from her lips.

"Say it again."

"Please."

He licked his lips and shook his head. "No, my name."

"Ton—" He took command of her lips before she finished. They were out of breath and trembling when he pulled back. "We're going to finish this in my room. I want you in my bed. You have five minutes, or I come find you." Dani blinked as he stepped back. Was he serious? His gaze roamed over her as he calmed his breath and righted himself, a hand forcefully adjusting the erection in his pants.

He swallowed hard. "Suite 102." He took her panties from the floor and put them in his pocket. "I'll be waiting," he said, looking into her eyes.

The door closed behind him. She felt cold suddenly, and quickly put on her bra and her dress, zipping it up just enough to keep it on. Her heart still pounded as she slipped her shoes on, and when she walked out the door, a bottle of champagne in hand, she could feel the naked heat he'd left between her legs.

She stepped back into the kitchen and made her way past the bar where a few people still lingered. Her heels struck the walkway from the winery to the resort accommodations. She fingered the palm leaves that grew out into the pathway.

It wasn't like her to sleep with someone she'd known

for such a short time. She could go back to her room and avoid the morning after, she thought. But what fun would that be? She could still taste the whiskey that lingered on his kiss, and her nipples still ached against the satin of her dress. He'd started a fire within her, and she wanted him to put it out.

Room 102 marked a white door in gold letters. She raised her fist to lightly knock. Shirtless and eager, Toni ripped open the door and pulled her into his dimly lit room. She kept a tight grip on the bottle as he picked her up, to her delight, and plopped her on the bed.

Light music played and she caught a clean musky scent in the air. The room was similar to hers; king-size bed, large bay windows overlooking the ocean, and glass sliding doors.

He kissed her as he peeled her out of her dress and unsnapped her bra, his gaze flaring when her breasts tumbled out. In seconds she was naked and staring up at the angular planes of his handsome face.

Toni kissed her again, and then pulled back. "Now tell me what you want."

She didn't even have to think. Dani positioned her legs on either side of him. "I want you inside me."

He thrust against her in answer. "I think I can handle that."

Toni whipped his belt to the floor; at the same time Dani tore at his pant buttons. She ripped his pants down and she came out of her skin at the sight of him hard and throbbing in boxer briefs.

"Touch me," he commanded low.

She cupped him, but it wasn't enough. She reached inside the waistband and grasped him firmly, feeling how warm and ready he was to give her what she was almost begging for.

His head rolled back as she slowly stroked. "That's good," he breathed, his body a pillar of lean rigid muscle. Before he was too far gone, Toni gently cradled her face and pulled her up to meet his body. He nudged her knees apart and gazed down at her with heavy-lidded blue eyes. His fingertips ran down her slick folds, rubbing and sliding over her, making her moan and quiver.

"You are so beautiful. So sexy," he breathed. Dani shuddered, her body ready for release.

"Now, Toni," she panted. "Please."

Toni reached past her and pulled a gold-foiled condom from atop the nightstand, quickly rolling the latex in place. Then all thoughts vanished when he palmed her thigh and slid deep inside her in one swift motion, thick, heavy and hard. Dani clawed at his shoulders as he pulled back slowly and drove home again, and again and again. She moaned as he continuously filled her, overwhelmed by his size and strength, but eager to take everything he was giving.

Dani undulated under him, coaxing rough grunts from him, nipping at his mouth with each thrust. Tremors wracked her, her legs falling open farther as he caged her with his body and slid in deeper. Dani felt her muscles clench around him and her heart started pounding out of her chest. She thrust up and held on to him as she came, vaguely aware of his lips on hers, and the sound of his rough cries against her mouth.

Chapter 3

New York

One year later

"Service!" Dani screamed from behind the chef's counter where she was meticulously preparing Andre's special plate—veal shank with saffron infused risotto. The wait-staff within earshot paused at her shrill voice, then quickened their pace to grab the two entrées sitting idle under the heat lamp. She understood the confusion; technically she was "off," allowing Michele, her sous-chef, a crucial step in his training—running a Friday night dinner service.

"Feel the rhythm of the kitchen, Michele. You're behind, which makes them—" she pointed to the servers "—behind. Step it up." The young man gave Dani a solemn nod and a "yes, Chef," then barked his own orders.

Chef Andre Pierre may be the owner and famous face attached to the restaurant, but Dani had built the kitchen of Via L'Italy into a two-star Michelin rated powerhouse of culinary masterpieces, and wasn't going to stop until she got a third star.

Of course, if she and Andre landed the TV show they pitched to the Food Network, she'd no longer be worrying about that star. The world would see her cooking beside Andre, instead of behind him. Ghost chef… Dani could barely stand the term. Andre was the great and powerful Oz of the culinary world, while she was the little guy behind the curtain making it all happen.

She had tried to leave and pursue her own restaurant

once, but Andre increased her salary and made it worth her while to stay. When they got their first Michelin star, she got paid even more. On paper, she was successful. In real life, she felt like she was achieving none of her goals.

Dani no longer wanted to be a ghost chef in Andre's kitchen, or in his bed. They'd become more public with their relationship, meaning some of the staff knew, but she still got the feeling Andre was fighting boyfriend status. Her schedule was more grueling than his and they never saw each other much outside of the restaurant. But they made sense together. Slowly but surely, Dani knew that Andre would one day see that they made a good team.

"Is that for Andre?" Michele said, his voice always turning a bit acid when he mentioned Andre's name.

"Yes, I'm going to the office to cheer him up. He's been sulking since he got back from the network. I'm nervous he got bad news."

Dani slipped off her apron and ventured toward the dining room, skirting whizzing servers and bussers. All greeted her with a respectful "Chef." Andre's back office was empty. She passed by the storage alcove where the coats were lined and found a few had fallen from the rack. A muffled sound came from the closed storage door.

She moved forward, her hand on the knob when an audible moan was heard. He heart hammered, afraid to see what she knew was coming. Quietly she turned the knob. Andre was inside with Bette, their hostess. His back was to the door, pumping hard as she lay on the cluttered desk with her dress raised and her legs spread.

"You're going to be a star, baby girl," Andre gritted out in between thrusts.

The young hostess's eyes were closed, and then they fluttered open and found Dani. The girl yelled in horror, which didn't stop Andre's furious thrusts until she hit at him and pushed away.

He was breathing heavily when he snapped his head around to gaze at Dani. The hostess shoved her dress down and scurried past Dani into the hallway. Andre's shoulders slumped and he zipped up his pants. But what she saw in his eyes was not an apology. It was resignation. "I'm sorry you saw that. But what did you expect?"

Dani's eyes narrowed. "I expected loyalty."

"We never see each other. I can't even remember when we kissed last."

"We kissed this morning in bed."

"That goodbye kiss you gave me at 4 a.m. when you went to the fish market?"

Dani took in a deep breath. "Your customers are loving the fish."

"All you care about is the kitchen. Anywhere we go, anything we do, you end up at the kitchen."

"This is a 24/7 job as you well know. And it's not my kitchen, Andre, it's your kitchen. I am doing this for us!"

"No, you're not. Your focus, your drive…it's for you, Dani. You have no insecurities in the kitchen."

Insecurities? Dani's hands perched on her full hips. "What the hell does that mean?"

"It means all you think about is the kitchen. It's where you have control."

Dani rolled her eyes. She didn't need to listen to psychobabble from a cheater and a liar. What she did need was to find out what happened at the network.

"And what about the show, Andre? Does that get thrown away along with our relationship too?"

"They want to do it—" he paused "—but they want someone else to cohost. Someone with a millennial appeal." He had the decency to look apologetic.

"I'm thirty-three, Andre. I *am* a millennial."

"They want someone…like…a model or something."

"Ohhh, now I get it. I'm too fat to be on your show."

He slowly shook his head. "It's not my decision, Dani."

She cut him off. "And who is going to cook for you? The model that… Wait a minute, is Bette going to be on the show?" If anyone wanted to be a star, it was that woman that ran out of the room with her skirt up.

Andre's eyes hit the floor in answer.

"How long have you been screwing her?"

"Does it matter? We weren't exclusive."

She didn't think her heart could sink any lower. She refused to cry, replacing the emotion with pure anger.

Andre's voice turned to syrup. "Look, let's be adults about this. The show still needs you. *I* still need you. She'll be the face, but it will be your food. You'll get paid more than her, I'll see to that."

Her gaze went hazy. He wanted her to be a ghost chef for his new girlfriend?

"Fuck you, Andre." She threw the plate of food at his feet.

He jumped as it crashed and spilled, his gaze holding a challenge she wasn't interested in meeting.

He was predictable. She mused that she had been waiting for this moment, and now that it had happened, she had a kitchen to run. She turned and let the door close behind her, muffling whatever rant he was shouting at her back. She no longer cared. Actually she felt relieved. Wondering when he would screw up was a drain.

Her mother had always told her she played the game of love wrong, that she loved the men more than they loved her. She had fallen in love with Andre, she thought.

Michele was waiting for her when she walked back into the kitchen. His eyes fixed on her face. Did he know? A quick glance around the room caught raised eyebrows and concerned gazes. Did everyone know?

"Everything all right, Chef?"

She nodded with a neutral expression, alluding to nothing. Images of Andre and the hostess flashed in her mind. The other woman stood at her post smiling, welcoming a couple and ushering them to their table. Her dress was in place and her makeup was flawless. The man checked out her size four frame as she walked.

Dani cringed, fighting the urge to pull Bette's weave out in the dining room.

She decided to leave instead. Her presence was undermining Michele's practice. This was his night, his initiation into the wonderful world of chefdom. Should she tell him he'll never have a life? That his partner will get mad and leave him? Because running a kitchen was like being the head of a family, and you don't abandon your family, not even for love.

Dani made busywork of tasting the sauces. She turned to find the pasta and almost walked straight into Andre.

Get out of my kitchen! She cleared her throat. "Yes?"

"Since my dinner is on the floor, I'd love a plate of… whatever."

"Of course." Dani loaded a plate with penne, then drizzled the garlic and oil. "I suggest a white wine with this."

Andre looked at her for a long moment, and then scanned the room of staff that were working and simultaneously watching under their lids.

"Thank you." He nodded, then jammed a fork into the pasta and into his mouth. "Mmm" came from his throat. Then his face scrunched. "That's too much garlic."

A tidal wave of anger hit her.

"How dare you come into my kitchen and insult this food! Do you have any idea what I have done for you? Do you think you could have made two stars with that bull you were serving three years ago? You would have been closed had it not been for me!" Her voice cracked. The staff stilled. She grabbed the plate from his hands and tossed it on the counter. "I hope she was worth it," Dani spit.

Dani turned on her heel and found her bag under the counter. Then she stomped to the wall and grabbed her coat. She hugged Michele and held him at arm's length. "Michele, you're ready." Dani had to look away when his face drained of all color. He'd be fine. They all would. She trained them well.

She stepped toward the door but stopped when she saw movement in the dining room. It was Bette, opening a bottle of wine, laughing with a young couple. Dani found herself next to the hostess, startling the girl midpour.

"Your pour should be just less than half the glass." Dani grabbed the stem of the glass and tossed the ruby liquid in the girl's face. Her squeal mingled with the collective gasp of the room. Rivulets of red dripped from her chin. "See, too much." Dani set the glass down in front of the gawking couple and executed a perfect pour, then held it up. "Now, this is a glass of wine." Dani splashed the second glass in Bette's face, this time hitting the dinner guests.

"You fat bitch!" The girl's tears were pink.

Dani shivered with rage at the word. "I'd rather be fat and smart, than skinny and stupid."

Andre appeared, wrenching the wineglass from Dani's hand and apologizing over and over to the couple.

"He's all yours," Dani said to the girl.

Dani felt the eyes of the room as she marched toward the front door. Skirting waiting couples, she pushed through the door and hailed a cab downtown, watching the city smear by.

She walked into her apartment like seeing it for the first

time. It was a mess, like her life. She picked up her phone and dialed Nicole, but got no answer. Then Liz, again no answer, but a text came through saying she was on a date and would call later. Her father, a fashion photographer turned tattoo artist, was backpacking through Asia. She scrolled through her phone and stopped at Mom. Her thumb hesitated. It was almost ten at night in LA. She was sure her mother would be getting ready for bed, if not in bed already. The woman had a regimen stricter than a marine. Dani dialed, sure her mother wouldn't pick up.

She's not going to answer, Dani thought, debating if she should hang up. Maybe it was a sign, emotional conversations with her mother didn't usually make her feel better. She'd thrown that tidbit in her mother's face once during an argument, to which her mother had calmly replied, *I'm not like other mothers*.

The second her mother answered, the tears she was holding back slid down her face in hot streaks. "Mom," she choked out.

"Danica, you know I'm about to go to bed. I need twelve hours or…" She paused. "What on earth—" A half sigh. "Are you crying?"

It was the exasperated sigh that pulled Dani from her fetal position on the couch. She dabbed at her eyes and wiped her nose with a tissue, then took a calming breath. Her mother never stood for such theatrics, even though she was still the most dramatic woman Dani had ever known.

"Yes." Dani swallowed. "It's been a rough night." Dani heard rustling in the background and imagined her mother in a face mask and silk head wrap resting in her king-size bed.

Although her mother was still considered a supermodel, at fifty-five years old—sixty-five if you paid attention to birth certificates—Francesca Watts was rarely offered work anymore, but she still treated every night like she was waking for a photo shoot the next day.

"Well, do I have to guess what happened or are you going to tell me?"

"I quit the restaurant."

"Good, now you can start your own. I'm sure Daddy would give you the money." Dani noted that her mother didn't offer. She also wasn't sure either of them had that type of cash just lying around anymore.

Dani sniffed. "That's not all." Dani made it through the abbreviated story of her breakup with Andre without another wave of tears.

"He wasn't strong enough for you, dear, I told you that. Not many men can handle women like us."

It was the same thing she said to Dani after her father had left and moved back to Sweden. Dani began to think the call was a mistake.

"Mother, just once I'd appreciate a little sympathy. I just want a virtual hug and for you to tell me it's going to be okay."

"Well, if you had moved to California with me instead of choosing to be nearer to your father, then I'd be able to hug you in person and do *all* of that."

"That is *not* the reason I stayed, Mother. I chose my career over the *both* of you—it just happened to be in New York."

"And now you're crying."

"There is no correlation." Dani quelled her rising voice and shook her head. "God, why can't we have a conversation like normal people?"

"Normal people?" her mother sneered. "We are *not* normal. Normal people aren't Michelin-starred chefs, Danica. I made love to David Bowie, for God's sake."

Dani chuckled as she cringed, feeling a little better.

Her mother actually sounded proud of her. "Please, I can't handle that story now."

"Yes. Yes. Now stop this crying. Did you get the dress I sent you?"

"It's too small."

"Well, did you gain more weight?"

And that lovely feeling came crashing down. "I don't know, Mother, I don't weigh myself on a daily basis like you do."

"Well, that designer runs a bit bigger, I thought it would fit."

"I'm fat, Mother, get over it."

"You're not fat, you're full figured. Lots of women would kill for your hourglass shape. Women are paying thousands of dollars to achieve your natural breast size, my dear. But now that you're done with that backbreaking job you can go back to Pilates."

Her mother's personal trainer had almost killed her one summer. She'd only lost a pound.

"No, thanks." Dani sipped a glass of wine, trying to ignore the fact that her mother still thought of her as someone who just needed to work out a little more and *poof*, she'd be a size four. "*She* called me fat."

"Who did?"

"The hostess Andre is cheating with."

"And did you tell that hood rat that she was just a sex toy?"

Dani laughed then. She knew her mother had issues about her weight, but she never allowed another person to say so.

"I'm glad you're laughing. Now, pull yourself up and take one step forward. You'll figure out what to do. I have to go."

Dani frowned. "Early breakfast with that old Persian billionaire?"

"No, darling, that ended months ago. I'm on my way to Milan tomorrow."

At the mention of Milan, Toni's firm lips and lean body popped into her mind. She ran a hand over her hair and shook the vision away. "Oh. Why?"

"I'm in a campaign for Chanel. Ageless, timeless, something or other. It was a cat fight between Naomi and me, God forbid they have two African American models in the campaign, but they chose me." She waited a beat. "I was the first black model to walk in Paris, you know."

Dani knew. She'd heard all of her mother's groundbreaking stories. Had seen all of the pictures of her slim, satin-skinned mother gracing magazine covers.

Her mother's success had been a series of highs and lows, with more and more lows as the gracefully aging beauty got older.

"That's great, Mom. Why didn't you mention anything?"

"You know how this goes. I'll get there and they may not even use me."

"So it's like a test thing?"

"Mmm…something like that."

Dani couldn't imagine the blow to her mother's ego. It was a go-see. An audition.

"They'll be idiots not to use you."

"Yes. They would." Her mother seemed to hesitate. "Would you like to come? It's been a while since we were in Milan together. I can get us a suite at the Baglioni."

"You want me to come with you?"

"Well…yes. Why not? You're not working." Dani blinked, intrigued, but unsure if that was a good idea. The last time Dani had been invited to one of her mother's shows had been during Milan Fashion Week when she was eight. The nanny canceled and the hotel staff couldn't watch her, so her mother had to take her along.

You do not make noise or speak, Francesca had insisted in the limo to the photo shoot. *I'm going to put you in my dressing area. And if anyone asks you who you are, you do not say a word. You run and hide. They might think you're a homeless Italian child and just leave you alone.*

But I want to see the cameras.

No. Francesca had sent her a look that could melt steel.

Why?

Because your mother needs to protect her image. Dani hadn't known what that meant, she'd just known Mom meant business.

As the pair ran unnoticed into the dressing room, Dani thought of the whole thing as a game. But when Dani had laughed a little too loud, she had seen that look on her mother's face and shut it down. Dani didn't know how long she had been in the dressing room by herself, but the thought of the cameras was too enticing. She'd tiptoed behind some tall equipment in her little Keds and ran into a king's spread of food. Sandwiches, cheeses, grapes and…cookies!

Dani was stretched over the lip of the table when her mother's makeup artist had found her with her fingers curled around a macaroon.

Bella? *Dov'è tua madre?* Dani had turned to run but she knocked over a microphone stand. *Francesca, do you know this child? I asked her where is her mother, but I think she's mute.*

Heads swiveled between Dani and her mother. The little girl flinched when Francesca's eyes sparked with split-second rage. Her mother turned to her makeup artist.

Robbie, do I look like I've had a child?

Roberto waved his brushes in the air. *Of course not. I doubt your baby would be so...robust.*

The room laughed.

That is just baby weight, her mother had quipped, *but... I'm sure she must be with one of the production managers or something.* She'd narrowed her eyes at Dani. *Would you like an autograph, sweetie? How about you sit quietly in my chair over there and I'll give you one when I'm done. Okay?*

Roberto had left Dani by the table. *You are so charitable, Francesca.*

I try to give back whenever I can, Robbie.

Never would Dani forget that day, or ask to go to work with her mother again. But she wasn't a kid anymore, maybe this time it would be fun.

"You'll be able to see Marcello," Francesca sighed. Dani heard the jealous sound of her mother's voice. Not long after Dani's first and last time going to a photo shoot, her mother again couldn't find a sitter, and dropped Dani off in the hotel restaurant.

Chef Marcello Farina, her old mentor and owner of three-Michelin-star rated Via Carciofo where she trained, had found her in the corner, put her in a white coat and gave her odd jobs around the kitchen. She had loved it. Marcello was like a second father, and probably the reason she was a chef.

"Just say yes already. I have to sleep," Dani's mother said at the tail end of a yawn.

Maybe talking to Marcello would give her some perspective, Dani thought. What could it hurt? "Okay, I'll go."

Chapter 4

New York

Toni sank into the back seat of the car service and watched out the window as they sped up the West Side Highway. The call he'd gotten from Louis, the manager of his Upper West Side warehouse, had been frantic, making it necessary for him to interrupt his trip to JFK Airport. He checked his Omega timepiece and estimated that he had a little over an hour to fly standby on the next flight.

Street vendors doled out coffee to groggy workers while children were dragged by the hand into prestigious-looking school buildings. It was a sharp contrast to the slick glittering nightlife where the drinks were just as cool as the people. He sighed, disappointed that he had to cut his trip short.

He'd called his daughter yesterday to wish her a good night and found that his ex-wife had left Sophia home alone again. Yes, at thirteen years old his daughter could take care of herself, but it was the way she was taking care of herself that worried him. A boy had answered Sophia's phone when he'd called.

Since he'd moved out over a year ago, she stayed with him every other week, which gave him limited glimpses into her life. The weeks she was with him she was an angel—if teenagers could ever be angels. She was safe and out of trouble at least. But the weeks with her mother, like this week, had become increasingly problematic. He blamed it on Ava's new boyfriend and her penchant for going out more than staying home.

The second the call picked up he'd heard a chorus of

"shhhs" followed by the lowering of music. She had been having a party. Girlfriends doing makeup and watching movies, he presumed. Then a deep voice said her name. He recalled the conversation like it was happening all over again.

"Papà?" Her voice was apprehensive.

"Why is a boy answering your phone?"

"He was just being stupid, Papà. It's not what you think."

"It better not be what I think, Sophia. Where's your mother?"

"Um—" giggles in the background "—upstairs in the bath?"

"Go get her."

"She'll be mad if I interrupt."

"Stop lying to me. I'm calling her right now."

"No, don't! Okay, she's not here. She's out with Bruno. But she'll be back later. I'm fine."

"Who is there watching you?"

"I don't need a chaperone, Papà. It's just a few friends, we're watching a scary movie."

"You hate scary movies."

"Not anymore." He bet that boy just loved scary movies.

"I want everyone out of that house and I'm sending Nonna to check on you," he said over her whining protests. "I'm coming home tomorrow and we are going to discuss this with your mother when I get back."

After a quick call to his mother, she agreed to drive the twenty minutes from her country home into the city. He sent a scathing text to Ava and received no response. Yeah, the three of them were going to have a serious sit-down when he got home. Toni sighed his frustration just as the car pulled into the shipping lot behind the warehouse. He jumped out and quickly crossed to the large building.

Toni heard the echo of the argument the minute he

walked through the freight entrance. Skirting trucks and small forklifts, he propped his bags on a tall stack of wine crates and shouted hello to the operations manager, who stopped his crate packing and jerked his head in the direction of the commotion. Toni quickened his pace to the front of the store.

Andrea Gomez of Star restaurant group had shown up expectantly without an appointment and, by the way her voice was rising, seemingly irate. Toni stopped just at the threshold to button his suit jacket, then realized with a sigh that he wasn't wearing it, opting for only a navy T-shirt and trousers for his trip back to Milan.

He debated running back to the town car sitting idle in the shipping lot, then thought against it. There was no time. He needed to catch that earlier flight, needed to get home to his daughter. A shrill female voice pulled him over the threshold into their show and tasting room.

"Do you hear what I'm saying? I'll pay retail if I have to, just get me something that won't embarrass me!" Andrea's hair was wild and she had both of her hands on the counter as if she was going to jump over it. The wineglasses lined up on the tasting bar trembled, as did Louis, who had taken a step back and was clutching the bottle in his hand like a life raft.

"Andrea," Toni said, his arms wide and voice jubilant, making sure to pronounce her name with extra Italian flair. "On-dre-uh," a sexier spin on the American "Ann-dree-uh." He kissed her on both cheeks.

"Antonio! Oh, I had no idea you were in town." Andrea immediately straightened and jammed her fingers through her hair.

Louis visibly relaxed.

"When I heard you were here, I had to come. You look ravishing." Andrea's lids fluttered and she shifted ner-

vously in her big coat, sweatpants and Uggs. It was almost
10 a.m. and Toni could only assume Andrea was not having a good morning.

Toni took her shaky hand in his, steadying her erratic
behavior and demonstrating that the drunken kiss she'd laid
on him several months ago at a wine conference in Verona
did nothing to harm their business relationship. Not that he
would have minded a night with her, but he never mixed
business with pleasure. "I was only here a few days. I'm
on a flight back this morning. Now, *bella*, what has happened that has you in such a state?" He was laying it on
thick, but if he was going to get this done in ten minutes,
he needed her attention.

"I'm hosting a wedding tonight for the mayor's daughter at John-Duc and those Figgertons sent me cases of
spoiled wines. They are like vinegar! This is the mayor's
daughter—it could ruin me!" Andrea's face reddened with
every word.

Toni knew the Figgertons well. A distributor of self-
proclaimed "elegant" wines from smaller less known vineyards. Which appealed to a hipster sensibility of indie
winemaking, but Toni knew it really meant the wines were
less traceable, amateur at best and definitely not worth the
price he knew Andrea had paid.

"You know I would have come to you, Toni, but she's
a vegan hippie and insisted on small vineyards, as if this
woman knows anything about wine, and—"

Toni stopped her and urged her to take a deep breath.
His specialty was in fine wines from more established vineyards, vintners he knew personally. All had a reputation for
the highest quality grapes, rich terroir, flawless production
and generations of knowledge. It was a combination you
could actually taste.

And as their distributor, he made sure they got the price they deserved. Discounts were for the Figgertons.

She was looking at him with doe eyes, as if she wanted to apologize for going somewhere else. It didn't bother him that she didn't come to him first. In fact, he was elated that he found an opportunity to kill two birds with one stone. Toni was personally representing his friend's rebuilt winery in Brazil. Getting it in front of the mayor could be excellent for business.

"Louis, bring the Deschamps."

"But, sir—"

"I know, Louis. Let's have a taste." Louis darted to the back and Toni watched Andrea's gaze travel down his front. He inwardly urged Louis to hurry.

"So." Andrea stepped forward, letting her coat fall open to reveal a white low-cut T-shirt, with a tiny coffee stain on the front. "How have you been?"

Louis had a new glass on the bar and a bottle of Deschamps Cab Franc open and poured in seconds. Andrea looked at the bottle, then at Antonio.

"This is a Deschamps. I can't do a fine wine, the bride will never go for it."

"This one is from the smaller biodynamic vineyard in Brazil."

Andrea gasped. "Didn't they have a fire?"

"Yes, but they have risen out of the ashes like a phoenix. Taste it." Toni leaned in as she lifted the glass to her lips. "There is a story in that wine any hippie would love."

Andrea swallowed and tried to hide her satisfaction, a tactic he knew she used for negotiation, but Toni had seen the pleasure in her eyes. She signaled for one more taste, which Toni approved by a slight nod.

"Hmm," was all she said as she stared at the bottle. The

forest green label etched in gold writing with trademarks and family seals meant…*cha-ching*.

Andrea was still trying to play it cool, but her Uggs were shifting. "Is this all you have to show me?"

"Of course not, but I think it's what you need to make your bride happy."

"How much is in the back?"

"Enough for a wedding of, say, four hundred." Louis began to fidget, wide-eyed.

"Price?"

Toni stepped forward, his smile on full wattage. "*Bella*, for you? I'll make you a deal."

Minutes later Toni was in the back grabbing his bags. The pit stop ran later than expected, but he still might be able to just make his flight. He breezed by his operations manager. "Marco that entire palate goes to Jean-Duc on Park Avenue right now." Marco and his staff stopped packing the crate and frowned.

Louis skidded to a halt. "But we are shipping this to Bagatelle Miami tonight! And we have none left in the other warehouses."

"I'll call Destin, Louis. We'll ship straight from his cellar in Brazil. I'll call you later."

Toni climbed into the car and shut the door, nodding at Louis's anxious wave. He'd just sold more than expected of his friend's wines and made a fortune on the up-charge he slid by Andrea. He should be happy, but all he could think about was getting home.

With literally minutes to spare, Toni stepped onto the boarding dock and heard the doors close behind him. Someone upstairs was looking after him today. He found his seat in first class and then placed his laptop bag on the floor, along with the several gifts he bought for Sophia.

"Coffee?" He took the cup and thanked the stewardess,

then settled into the leather seat. He was about to put in his earbuds when a gray sweatshirt landed in the empty seat and he heard a soft thank-you to his right. A woman was standing by the seat, her arms extended as she rummaged in the overhead compartment. Her generous breasts quivered under her V-neck T-shirt which was tucked into a pair of high-waisted jeans.

Toni unfolded himself carefully from his seat, about to offer his help, when the woman slammed the compartment shut. He dragged his gaze from the curve of her hips in anticipation of seeing her face. He was met with large black sunglasses and a waterfall of dark hair that fell into her face and past her shoulders.

He folded himself back into his seat, still on alert if she needed anything. He decided to mind his own business, when a light pleasant fragrance teased his nose. From the corner of his eye he could see her twisting her hair into a ponytail, lifting her torso and chest up and out, and he found himself captivated. What was it about the way a woman moved?

Feeling like a pervert, he grabbed his coffee, only to glance back when he noticed her looking his way. She smiled. He smiled back, and then the pilot began to speak and the cabin readied for takeoff. The woman was lovely, but his thoughts had traveled to mocha-colored skin and floral tattoos. An occurrence that happened randomly and more frequently as the months went by. He assumed it was because his personal life had become a source of frustration. Dating wasn't going as well as he'd hoped. He mused that he was no longer just looking for love; he was looking for a life partner. Stability. One who could also love his daughter and deal with his ex. It raised the stakes, and kind of killed the romance of it all.

When had love gotten so complicated? And when had

he become so jaded? The old him would be flirting with his flight companion, instead he was avoiding her eyes.

The small cries of Dani's orgasm rang in his ear and he downed another sip of his coffee He wished he could have seen her during this trip to New York City. He'd gotten in three days of work and a few visits to his favorite haunts, but today had been the day he looking forward to the most. He'd made his reservation at Via L'Italy months ago. Yes, it was one of the best restaurants in the city, but he was more interested in seeing Danica again and that was where she worked. He smiled as his thoughts drifted to their delicious night of champagne and sex almost a year ago. Waking up alone the next morning had been a jolt to his ego, but he wouldn't change a thing about that night.

There'd been no rhyme or reason for his planned visit. He understood that she could be seeing someone, hell, he'd been dating quite a bit, but his intentions were not to have another one-night stand. He just wanted to see her.

Unfortunately he had to skip that reservation.

Toni began to feel very tired then. He didn't know what he was going to say to Ava when he got home, not that she'd listen, but he had hours to figure it out.

Toni fished his phone from his pocket to turn it off and found three messages from his mother. Each was an update on their new restaurant project Via Olivia, a farm-to-table dining experience just outside of Milan, along with a list of things he needed to accomplish when he got back.

For generations, his family has been in the wine and restaurant business. There were no titles or job descriptions, just his mother, the matriarch of their large family, telling everyone what to do. If you were in the family, you worked for the family. Strangely enough it was successful. Lorenzetti restaurant group owned several restaurants throughout Italy, including a three-Michelin-starred restaurant in the center of Milan run by his uncle.

Although Toni had his wine business, he was also an active partner in the restaurant group. While he had a small stake in all of the restaurants, this new venture had been his idea. Five years of landscaping, gardening, designing the perfect villa, he had invested a lot of time and money into making it a success. And with his uncle overseeing the menu, Toni knew it would be *fantastico*. Just a week or two now and they would be open.

He quickly texted his mother back, then balked at the last text that came through.

Ava still hadn't arrived home.

Toni turned off his phone and pinched his nose, praying the plane could make warp speed.

Chapter 5

Milan

Dani arrived at the Baglioni Hotel Carlton in the early morning but her mother had already left for work. A little jet-lagged, she ordered up a sizable pot of coffee and some pastries to the two-bedroom suite, then unpacked her toiletries and an outfit for the day. After some digging in her bursting bag, she hung up a dress in the closet for later, then decided that unpacking the rest of her bag could wait.

The rainfall shower in the black marble spa bathroom made her seven-hour red-eye worth it. She began to feel like a human again as the water slid over her skin. *Milan.* She hadn't been back in years, not because she didn't want to, but because running a kitchen in New York had proven as consuming as Chef Marcello had promised. Knowing Marcello was working, she planned to surprise him later that night and maybe get some life advice too.

Dani toweled off and let the high-thread-count towels caress her skin, lingering over her sensitive breasts as images of Toni Lorenzetti naked and thrusting into her took over her thoughts. Even as she and Andre had committed to each other—she'd thought—flashbacks of Toni were a spontaneous occurrence that she couldn't help. Someone would smile and she'd see Toni. A tall man would walk through the door at the restaurant, she'd see Toni. She'd hear an accent, any accent. Toni. She chalked it up to the great sex because what other explanation could there possibly be?

He was here in Milan, she thought. She exited the bathroom and sat on the bed, running complimentary lotion over her legs. The soft duvet reminded her of the duvet they'd had no use for in Brazil. She'd woken up groggy from the champagne, her body aching from the high-octane sex, and warm from the humidity of the air and the heat of his body. She had slid from underneath his heavy arm, almost tripped over the pile of sheets on the floor, found her clothes and tiptoed out the door, and back to reality.

You could call it a walk of shame, but she hadn't been ashamed. It had been a perfect night and she didn't want the memories ruined by an awkward morning after. So she had left without saying goodbye to Toni Lorenzetti.

Which was why now, even in his gorgeous city, she wouldn't be saying hello.

Dani put on her robe and strolled out onto the terrace overlooking Via della Spiga, one of the best shopping streets in the city. Designer logos on the buildings glittered and beckoned while severely fashionable men and women were already on the streets. A woman in camel-colored leather pants strolled by. Dani felt envy prickle her chest; they probably didn't even make those in her size.

She hugged her robe closer, remembering that everyone in Milan looked and dressed like a supermodel. She recalled the suits hanging in Toni's room—Cavalli, Brioni, Armani, all custom. She shook her head at the obsessive thoughts of a man she hadn't seen in almost a year. She could see him with the girl wearing the leather pants, not with her. She was not fashionable, nor was she a supermodel. She was just a chef.

Or at least she used to be.

After a light lunch in the lobby, Dani strolled the marble streets, visited the La Scala theater, awed at the sidewalks filled with busy café seating and strolled by the cathedral— which always took her breath away.

Dani texted her mother to join her at Via Carciofo, but

her mother was already on her way to dinner with Chanel's people. That was a good sign. So Dani put on her black lace dress and her heels and ordered a car to the restaurant.

It had been almost eight years since Dani had worked as a sous-chef at Via Carciofo. It was still the most beautiful restaurant she had ever seen. Tucked away in a secluded courtyard of one of Milan's oldest hotels, vine-covered stone columns hid the small stairs that led to the mezzanine patio where twenty tables were perfectly staged with tea lights, white roses and fine china.

Back there time didn't exist, hence the ambiguous hours of operation—open at dusk. The lack of time limits only enhanced the romance. Reservations were recommended and hard to come by. Once you booked a table, it was yours for the night, no matter what time you got there. And the kicker? There was no menu.

Upon securing a reservation the hostess noted any allergies or preferences. Once recorded, Chef designed a seven-course prix fixe menu of his choosing paired perfectly with two to three wine recommendations. She had never seen one dish come back to the kitchen. In this space, eating was purely for pleasure.

Dani's heels clicked up the stone steps and she breathed in the fragrant pastel-colored lilies that lined the entrance. Easter was in a couple weeks and she made a mental joke that what she gave up for lent was her job. She slowed, wondering what to say to Marcello. How do you tell your mentor that you've given up on life?

The hostess was gracious when Dani told her she was just visiting Marcello and turned down her offer to be announced. Dani wanted her visit to be a surprise. She walked past the tables, glancing around to see if she recognized any of the servers. She didn't. Then she looked for Wendall, the maître d'hôtel of almost forty years, but he was nowhere to be found. Strange. He never left the dining floor.

Reaching the bar, she ordered a drink and asked the bartender to tell Marcello someone had a complaint. Game for a prank, the bartender went to the back. She smiled, anticipating Marcello's blustering red face. She heard a muffled crash of pots and pans and envisioned Marcello yelling at his staff. She smirked. She'd felt that rage and had given it to her own staff many times.

She turned to the packed tables to see if anyone else had heard. She saw only smiles and laughter while a bar back went table-to-table lighting the tea candles.

An audible shout came from behind the bar. Dani put down her drink and leaned over the bar. She spied someone sprint past the windows in the double doors. Something was wrong.

Dani pushed through the double doors. The wall of heat that assaulted her was forgotten when she saw the kitchen staff gathered around Marcello, who was laying supine on the floor in the bartender's arms. His right hand held his left arm close to him and his face was scrunched with pain.

Wendall stood to the side with a phone to his ear speaking in urgent Italian. Dani's Italian was rusty but she recognized the word for *hospital*.

"Signora, please. You cannot be in here." One of the staff came forward. Dani ignored him, trying to get her head around the fact that the man that had once been like a father to her was having a heart attack.

Amid quizzical looks, she dropped her clutch and dropped to her knees, taking Marcello's free hand.

"Marcello. It's Dani," she whispered through budding tears. He'd aged the superficial way men do. His hair was thinner and had turned white, but his face held few wrinkles.

Marcello pried his eyes open and they widened in recognition. His mouth hung slack with breaths and grunts. Dani could see him straining to speak, but he couldn't form the words. Medics burst through the back door.

Dani backed away as they huddled around Marcello armed with medical supplies. In seconds his black chef's coat was ripped open and monitors were attached to his chest. Dani feared the worst and wrung her hands as she prayed a silent prayer.

Servers came through the kitchen doors and stalled. No one moved as Marcello was strapped to a gurney and hooked to an oxygen tank. His eyes drifting open then closed. Dani watched the deep movement of his chest as they began to wheel him away.

As they passed by her, his arm shot out and swung at the air between them. She stepped forward, grasping his hand. His other pulled at the face mask.

"*Per favore*, I think he wants to say something," Dani shouted.

"Cuh…Cuh…" Marcello stuttered.

"Chef, stay calm. I'm coming to the hospital."

"Nuh." Marcello shook his head. "Kit-en."

Dani frowned. Kittens? "Marcello, put your mask back on. We can talk later at the hospital."

Marcello rapidly shook his head and a medic stepped forward.

"Step back, signora. We must get him to the hospital."

She did as she was told, watching the pointed look in Marcello's eyes. The medics were quick to restrain him and the mask was placed back on his face, but not before she heard him speak one last time.

"Kitchen."

The man was staring death in the face and he was concerned about the kitchen?

Wendall did a double take as he followed the gurney out

the back door. "Danica? Oh, Dani! My God, it's so good to see you." He ran over and gave her a quick hug. When he pulled back, tears sprang to his eyes. "They are taking him to Milan General. I must go with him. Please, find Gianni, the sous-chef. Please!"

"Go. I'll find him."

Just as quickly as they arrived, the medics and Wendall departed, leaving Dani and the staff bereft in their wake.

No one moved. The hostess cried. The line cooks blinked. The waitstaff were gaping from inside the double doors.

A burnt smell filled the room. Dani looked around and saw filets burning. Pots boiled over. A steak was sitting idle on a plate under the heat lamps. Vegetables lay midchop.

Kitchen.

Dani looked around the room for the sous-chef, who would be attired in black just as Marcello was, but she only saw white coats.

"Which one of you is the sous-chef?"

Heads swiveled, but no one came forward. She asked again, this time in her choppy Italian. "And get those fillets off the burners. Now." A line cook jumped.

The hostess came out of her stupor and raised her voice.

"Start shutting down. There will be no more service tonight. I'll inform our guests that we will be closed for the unforeseeable future and—"

"You will do no such thing," Dani interrupted.

"Signora, it seems you are a friend of the chef, but—"

"But nothing. Chef wants this kitchen open. And it will stay open. You have a room full of people out there expecting a Marcello Farina dining experience. Chef put his blood, sweat and tears into this restaurant. I'm not going to let you ruin that. I practically grew up in this kitchen, and I'm happy to stay and help. Now, where is your sous-chef?"

"Yes, where is Gianni?" the hostess asked the room.

"He's on break in the cellar," someone shouted.

"I'll get him," the hostess said, turning to leave. Dani stopped her.

"No, I'll get him. I know where it is." Dani had taken many breaks herself in the basement pantry. "You go out there and keep our guests happy."

The hostess gave Dani a wary look, then walked through the double doors.

"Start two new fillets and put a steak on the fly. I'll be right back."

Dani marched down the short hallway to the fridge, her mind racing with how to explain who she was and what happened to Marcello. She hoped the sous-chef could handle taking over the kitchen for a night. Or several nights if needed.

The cool air of the cellar was like a balm on her skin and she surveyed the frigid cuts of meat as she found her way around the shelving to the back.

"Ciao? Hello?" she called out. "Gianni? Oh, *scusa*," she apologized; startled when she found him bent over a rack. At first she thought he was gathering food, and then she saw the thin white line spread on the shelf and noticed the same powder dusted on his black coat.

He pinched his nose and looked at her quizzically. "*Scusami.* Are you lost?"

Dani blinked, trying to keep a lid on her emotions. If this were her kitchen, he'd be fired. And she doubted Marcello knew about this man's habits or he wouldn't be wearing that coke-dusted jacket.

But she didn't have time for morals and ethics. What she needed was a chef. Quickly she explained who she was and what happened, with Gianni seeming genuinely concerned.

Yet he balked when she asked him to run the kitchen, but then reluctantly agreed.

Gianni sweat bullets as he looked at the backup of orders. An erratic waitress burst into the kitchen needing her meals, her table was becoming belligerent. Then the hostess followed, with more problems.

"The key to the wine cellar is missing. I think Wendall had it." Dani knew that was where they kept the most expensive wines. What a disaster.

"Scusami," Gianni said with a sniff. The room watched Gianni put down the orders and walk out of the back door.

Dani looked around. "Did he just leave?"

The hostess's face drained of all blood.

Useless, Dani thought. She looked down at her cocktail dress, then grabbed an apron off the wall. Entrées began to fill her mind and she cursed the irony. Yesterday she quit this life, now she was thrust back in it. Taking a deep breath, she addressed the staff.

"Okay, first, my Italian is rusty. I need a volunteer to translate for those that do not speak English. *Grazie.* Consider yourself sous-chef," she said to the young man who raised his hand. "Second, someone needs to gather the orders that have come in so we can start at the top. Third, Marcello created something special here. We won't let him down tonight. My name is Dani, but tonight you can call me 'Chef.'"

Dani kicked off her heels and slid her feet into a pair of spare Crocs by the wall. She yelled out the first three orders to which she received a resounding "*Sì*, Chef."

Dani turned to the hostess. "What are we going to do about the wine locker?"

"I just called the owner. He should be here soon."

Immersed in her preparation of the dishes, a song played in her head as she chopped, sautéed, skewered and assembled each dish to an artful perfection. Her heart was pounding; she was sweating the edges out of her blowout and getting oil stains all over her dress.

But she also just pumped out three of the best entrées she'd ever created on the fly. Linguine con scampi, osso buco and risotto alla Milanese were prepared and served at lightning speed. She'd forgotten what it was like to cook like this.

Marcello had warned her about working for Andre. That he'd do none of the work and take all the credit. Those Michelin stars were hers and that poser knew it. But no one else did.

When the *mazzancolle* was ready she was bent over the plate, trying to ignore the crick that was building up on her neck. On a slow inhale she picked out the herbs and spices in the air. Saffron, cardamom, cumin, paprika, basil…a whiff of burned butter caught her nose.

"Who is watching the octopus?" she shouted.

"*Capito*, Chef!" came from behind.

The line cooks were pumping out dishes like crazy and servers were pouring complimentary champagne from the few bottles left in the fridge.

"Coming in!" A frantic server announced in an English accent as he burst through the kitchen door. He stopped just inside. "I've got a table asking for Lafite '82. Please tell me the cellar is open!" Dani sighed. It was a two-thousand-dollar bottle of wine and if that locker didn't open soon she had a feeling that all hell would break loose.

"Someone is coming," one of the line cooks shouted.

"Well, where are they?" the server repeated, running a hand through his perfectly gelled hair. He began to mutter softly, then grabbed his apron and chucked it to the floor. "I quit! I quit!"

Dani understood his tantrum. In this business your reputation was everything and losing a customer for whatever reason was bad for business.

"Coming in!" said a deep male voice. The door opened behind the irate server and Dani shot upright. Lean frame. Impeccable suit. Electric-blue eyes.

"Pick up your apron, Liam. I need to open the cellar and— Danica? Is it really you?" His eyes traveled over her, then a wide smile burst onto his face. "What is it with us and kitchens?"

Chapter 6

Dani picked her mouth up from the floor and froze. She couldn't believe that Toni was standing in front of her, and that his first image of her since the wedding was like this—frazzled and sweating.

"*Buona sera*, Chef. It's good to see you."

His voice washed over her and for a second she'd forgotten that they weren't the only two people in the room, until one of the line cooks jolted her out of her head.

"Chef? The *mazzancolle*?" The young man slid a plate in front of her and scurried away. She looked down at the bright orange prawns, then back to Toni.

"What… How… What are you doing here?"

"I could ask you the same."

Liam clapped his hands and steepled them as if in prayer. "But we have no time for reunions. Sir, please, my table."

Toni's curt nod was followed by a look Dani interpreted, as "we're not done." And by the aggressive way her blood was pumping through her veins, they weren't done. Not by a long shot.

Dani turned back to her dish, but her mind was on the man that was opening the wine locker. How did he have keys to Marcello's wine locker? More images of the two of them in Brazil had her sending out the dish with the server, then calling it back when she forgot the sprig of parsley. She needed to get it together. On a deep inhale she focused on the spices in the air again. Oregano, red pepper, sultry musk…huh?

Dani whipped around and there was Toni leaning against the stainless steel counter, his arms and ankles lightly crossed, smiling. He looked gorgeous, maybe a little leaner than she saw him last, but his facial hair was perfectly trimmed, his navy suit over the white T-shirt was impeccable and his sandy-blond hair was just the right kind of messy.

Liam was shouting a thank-you to the heavens and waving around bottles of Lafite.

She wanted to go to the bathroom and freshen up. She wanted to kiss that smile right off his face.

"How is this possible?" he said, his gaze roaming down her front, then behind her to the entrées at her back.

"You tell me. How do you have keys to Marcello's locker?"

"We own this restaurant. How are you standing here cooking for my guests?"

"I came to visit Marcello. What do you mean *we* own? This is Marcello's."

"And his family's. I am his nephew. How do you know him?"

"I used to be his sous-chef."

Toni jumped up. "Here? When?"

"It's been eight years now."

"I was in London at school then." Toni's eyes narrowed. "How did this never come up at the wedding?"

Dani's eyes darted around the room before she spoke.

"We didn't do much talking."

His wicked smile took Dani's breath away. "No, I guess we didn't." He shook his head. "I can't believe you are the one saving our asses."

"I can't, either," she said, grabbing the floral displayed artichoke she cut by hand.

"I don't know how to thank you." His tone turned serious. "He would have wanted—"

She shot upright, tears rushing to her eyes. "Oh God. Don't tell me—"

He grabbed her shoulders. "No, no, no…he's stable. My mother is with him." Dani sighed in relief. "I was saying he'd want to thank you himself. I'll be happy to take you to the hospital later."

People buzzed all around them, heat rose from the ovens and pots clattered on granite tops, but she felt the tension ease from her body and realized he was lightly rubbing his thumbs over her shoulders. It should have been awkward, but it felt grounding.

"Ahem!" They both stepped away from each other and turned their heads. A tense Liam stood on the other side of the kitchen counter.

"This reunion is lovely, really, but are any of these dishes mine?" Ignoring Toni, she bent over and worked quickly, handing Liam two plates and a "get the hell out of here" look. Liam studied the steaming plates, then gave her a once-over before loading them both on his arm.

Toni chuckled behind her. "Liam is our best server. His Instagram is full of our regular customers. They all ask for his table."

"He's intense." Dani stood and turned around, catching his gaze sliding back up to her face. She blushed and adjusted her dress, realizing that the skirt was probably riding up as she bent over.

"I've been thinking about you. It's good to see you," he said, the emphasis on *see*. Dani shivered, hoping she wasn't giving him "fuck me" eyes, because it was all she was thinking about.

"Coming in!" Another server burst through the doors, giving her a welcomed jolt.

She had to pull herself together. She had a kitchen to run. "Yeah, it's good to see you too. Look, I need to get back to work."

Toni clapped his hands. "How can I help?"

Her brows rose. In her experience, many restaurant owners did nothing but cash their checks. Kind of like Andre.

"I don't know, Toni, what can you do?"

"Where is Wendall?"

"He went with Marcello."

"Then it looks like I'm the new maître d'."

Toni straightened to his full height, buttoned his jacket, then tossed a white towel over his arm. He crossed the room in long easy strides and picked up a bottle of champagne. With the swift flick of his wrist, he popped the cork. It shouldn't have been sexy, but it was. Toni caught her gaze and winked before disappearing through the kitchen doors. Dani couldn't help it. She left her plates and peered out the small window to the dining room.

There was Toni, smiling, engaging customers, pouring champagne. The hostess was running a hand through her hair and righting her dress, watching him seductively. She walked back to her plates thinking that scene was way too familiar.

Movement in the corner caught her attention. Dani got closer and found a young slim girl with waves of dark hair fixated on the screen of her phone. Dani scrounged up some Italian.

"Scusami? Sei qui con qualcuno?"

Her head came up and electric-blue eyes appeared out of the dark curtain. "I'm waiting for my papà."

"Oh, where is he?"

She pointed to the dining room and Dani assumed he was a server. Quick flashes of memories assaulted her. Marcello standing over her with his hands on his hips, shaking his head when her mother begged him to watch her while she was at work. She mopped, she chopped, she was dead on her feet when her mother came back to the hotel. But Dani had loved it and volunteered to do it daily.

"Well, I don't allow loiterers in my kitchen. If you want to be here, you've got to help out."

Dani prepared for attitude. Instead the young girl turned off her phone and shrugged. *"Va bene."*

The hours went by quickly, with Toni being a gracious host and the kitchen pumping out seven courses of delight. His knowledge of wine was impressive, and unyielding, arguing with Dani over her recommendations for each dish. Finally she gave up, but she noticed he took one of her suggestions, conceding only with a slight nod. It reminded her of their first meeting and she schooled herself to concentrate.

It was two in the morning when the last customer left and Dani and her crew were scouring the grills, mopping the floors and wiping down the burners, all with the hope that Marcello would be all right and the kitchen would see another day.

Toni came through the doors carrying soiled linens and instructing the waitstaff to close up the dining room. He stopped when he saw her, threw the linens on the floor and pulled her into a bear hug. She kept her soapy hands in the air, but the rest of her body reveled in the feel of him. He pulled back slowly and looked into her eyes.

"Thank you."

"You're welcome."

He then turned to the whole staff and praised them, making everyone join in a round of applause. His gaze ran over the staff and paused.

"Sophia, are my eyes deceiving me? You are cleaning?"

The teen stood with a mop in her hand.

"You know her?" Dani asked.

"Come," Toni said to the girl, arm outstretched. Mop in tow, Sophia fit her slim frame against Toni's. "Dani, this is my daughter, Sophia. Sophia, this is Danica, a friend of mine and Marcello's."

Dani looked at Toni in wonder. He'd never mentioned a daughter, but she supposed she'd never asked. Suddenly the resemblance was uncanny. Sophia was tall for her age and those eyes were definitely his. She was going to be stunning, Dani thought.

"Nice to meet you, Sophia," Dani said as they politely shook hands. "Thanks for helping out."

"Now, I see you missed a spot over there," Toni teased Sophia, giving her a kiss on the head as the girl resumed mopping across the room. "How did you get her to clean?"

Dani shrugged. "I asked her."

"Humph," Toni said. Sophia always balked at chores.

"She's beautiful."

His smile was pride itself. "Yes, thank you."

"Do you have any more?"

"No." His head whipped around. "Do you?"

Dani shook her head, remembering that Andre didn't want kids, so she assumed she wouldn't have any. Now that things had changed, could kids be in her future? Her stomach made an embarrassing sound. Suddenly she was starving, since her plan to have dinner had turned into cooking dinner for fifty people.

"I'm starving. Have you eaten?"

Toni placed a hand over his stomach. "Not since lunch." He eyes darkened and he smirked. "Are you going to cook for me?"

Dani half smiled. He'd said the same thing at the wedding, but at the time her answer had been a resounding no. "I'm going to heat some things up for you. I think you've earned it."

"You honor me, Chef."

Fifteen minutes later, Dani heated up a simple pasta

marinara. Most of the staff had finished cleaning and gone, leaving Dani, Toni and Sophia to their late-night dinner. Toni's sounds of pleasure as he enjoyed her pasta assaulted her senses in a myriad of ways. She was pleased, a little too pleased, that he loved her cooking, but the sounds he was making were reminiscent of their night together. She was glad Sophia was there as a buffer.

"You can cook, Dani."

"Well, thank you, Toni. It's just marinara."

"I really like it too," Sophia chimed in, sitting on the island swinging her legs.

"Yes, but what's in it?"

"Well, I could tell you, but then I'd have to kill you."

Toni's eyes widened. "*Top Gun.* You just Top Gunned me."

Dani laughed. "I did. Sorry, Goose."

"Goose?" Toni's head jerked back. "Did you see me out there tonight? I was Maverick."

"I'm Maverick, obviously."

"That's ridiculous."

"What's a 'Maverick'?" Sophia asked, forking more into her mouth.

Toni swallowed. "It's an '80s film about fighter pilots."

"Oh! Yeah, I think I saw it with Mamma."

Dani noticed Toni's eyes darken a bit and she was reminded that he was divorced. A silence descended as the trio finished their meals. Dani stretched out her hand for their empty plates, but Toni took hers instead.

"The cook doesn't clean," he murmured, staring at her lips. She felt that look between her legs.

He and Sophia shared the sink and left their clean plates to dry in the rack. Then Toni tossed a towel on the counter and turned to both girls.

"I'm going to stop by the hospital. Who's game?"

"I am," Sophia shouted. All Dani saw were long legs and hair as Sophia gathered her things then disappeared into the bathroom.

"How is she not tired? She's lucky it's the weekend," Dani said to Toni with a smile.

Her smile faulted when she looked into Toni's eyes, something dark behind them. He glanced at the closed bathroom door, then came for Dani. In three strides he was in front of her, cupping her face, capturing her lips with his, his tongue commanding her own. The kiss was fire and burn, filled with months of pent-up longing, at least it was for her, but by the way he was eating at her mouth and pressing her body into his, she'd say if his daughter wasn't there, he'd have her back down and legs spread on the kitchen island.

He pulled his lips just inches from hers. "Are you seeing someone?"

"No," she whispered.

"Good."

They heard the door click and, just as quickly as the kiss started, it ended in a rush of breath and blinking eyelids. Toni pulled his body away from hers and walked calmly toward the door. Dani slowly turned around, acting like she was gathering towels when she was really trying to calm her breathing.

Sophia stood by the bathroom, her eyes darting between them. *"Pronto?"*

"Ready," Dani said under her breath.

Chapter 7

When Toni explained to the hospital staff that they were family, a kind nurse took pity and let them in Marcello's room. They were quiet, feeling better being by his side. But the stress of the day finally got to all of them, and one by one they all dozed in their chairs.

Dani woke and raised her head from the hospital wall. She blinked against the grogginess of jet lag and pure exhaustion from the night before. The room was dim, but a sliver of daylight shone through the closed curtains. Steps away, Marcello lay in a deep sleep hooked up to beeping monitors, and her mind ran through the events from the night before.

Marcello had almost died.

She relived seeing him lying on the floor and wheezing out the word *kitchen*. Was that what he cared about most? Dani thought back to what Andre had said to her, that all she thought about was the kitchen. That wasn't true...was it? Would she be dying on the floor one day using her last breath to say "kitchen"? Nothing about that thought was appealing.

Then there was Toni. *That kiss.* She turned her head and found him at the other end of the room slouched in his chair, his eyes closed and head resting on the wall. He was too tall and broad for the small metal frame and she suspected he'd be feeling pains in his back later. Sophia was curled up in the chair next to him, her body leaning into his. A protective arm was slung around her.

Long deep breaths came through his slightly parted lips, emphasizing his sensual mouth. He had a beautiful easy smile that had charmed even the hardest customer in the restaurant. By the end of the night everyone knew his name, and loved him.

Kind of like Andre, she winced. Charming the ladies right out of their pants.

But she hadn't expected Toni to be so competent and collected. Men like him wanted attention, nothing more. And yet he'd served more dishes and poured more wine than the staff. Eight hours on his feet without complaint. Andre never worked that hard a day in his life.

Are you seeing someone?

Grabbing her little bag she quietly found the bathroom and recoiled from her reflection. Her flawless night-out makeup had melted down her face, settling into creases around her eyes that didn't need to be emphasized. Baby hairs frizzed around her face. And her lips were drained of color.

And she smelled. She had worked too hard and long for there not to be a tinge of BO, but her beautiful dress had also absorbed every splatter and aroma from the kitchen. She pulled the soft band from her hair and shook out the waves over her shoulders. Yeah, her hair got it too.

Dani ran the hot water and prepared for a thorough whore's bath in the sink. She placed her hands under the water and pulled back at the sharp sting. Burns, she'd forgotten them. Tiny fresh marks from oil splashes and hot plates. They were a chef's badges of honor and she'd gotten used to them appearing in all sorts of places on her body, but she had no ointment to rub on them. Maybe she could trouble a nurse for some.

She pumped the little hospital soap dispenser and in only a few minutes she was fresh faced with her damp hair up and smelling like medical grade hospital soap rather than a garbage dump. Digging in her little clutch, she pulled out a nude lipstick and felt like a woman again with each glide over her lips.

Satisfied that she no longer looked like a zombie chef, she tiptoed back into the room intending to go into the hallway and call her mother. Instead she walked straight into Toni's solid chest.

He was gripping his phone and although it was still dark she could see the concern in his bright eyes. "Are you all right?" he whispered. Sophia and Marcello both still slept.

She nodded and held up her phone in silent communication. He nodded back and they both softly shuffled into the lit hallway.

"I need to call my mother," Dani said when the door shut behind them.

While she was working, her mother had sent several texts, the last one a sarcastic plea: You better be with a man.

She didn't know whether it was good or bad that after long absences her mother had never assumed she was dead or dying. Dani had "run away" when she was ten. It was Paris Fashion Week and in protest of being left again with the hotel housekeeper, Dani had run down to the parking garage and hid behind a cluster of bins. Where she fell asleep for hours.

Knowing she was in trouble, little Dani ran back to her hotel room and walked through the door to find the hotel manager, a policeman and the maid who was watching her—all sighs and relief to see her safe. The maid had actually dropped to her knees in tears.

Her mother? On the couch in her pink silk lingerie set and heeled slippers, reading the evening paper. Francesca had half lowered the paper and peered at Dani over a bent corner.

See, she's fine. Just out exploring. Thank you all so much for coming, but I must get some sleep. Dumbstruck, the group had filed out, but not before the maid kissed Dani on the head. Dani had bet she would make a good mother one day.

Alone in the room, neither moving from their prospective positions, Dani had crossed her arms. *You don't care about me!*

Of course I do, don't be ridiculous. And is that grease on your shirt? You better get in the shower before you come tracking all that stuff in here.

I could have been killed!

But you weren't.

Someone could have taken me!

Francesca had rolled her eyes. *This is Paris, not New York. There is no better place to get lost.*

You weren't even worried!

Her mother had stomped across the room in her heels and stood her five-foot-eight-inch frame in front of Dani. Dani had dropped her arms and prepared to run. *Did you see all of those people I called? Yes, I was worried, but stress lines on this face won't do, young lady. You are going to stop this nonsense. And that maid is going to be fired for letting you out of her sight.* Dani had gasped and run to her room.

"Hey, where'd you go just now?" Toni was standing close, his voice low and a frown on his handsome face.

"Sorry, I'm just tired."

"I bet. You were incredible last night. I don't know what we would have done had you not been there. Fate, no?"

She shook her head and shrugged. *Fate?* She'd just call it coincidence. "I'm just glad I could help."

"I was in New York recently. I had made reservations at Via L'Italy." His hands went into his pockets. "I wanted to say hello, but my plans got cut short." He frowned, trying to make sense of it. "And here you are, saving my family. I say fate. You must be some sort of angel."

She paused, glad he hadn't come to L'Italy, preferring he not know that she was a ghost chef. Or that she and Andre had been lovers.

"I'm no angel, Toni. I think you know that. I'm just a chef—who needs to call her mother." She lifted her hand and waved her phone. His hands flew from his pockets and grabbed her hand.

"Angel, what is this?"

"What? Oh, it's just a burn." She winced when he touched it. Then his hands ran up her forearm and over the colors of the tattoo, frowning at the bumpy texture of her skin there. The burn had been so bad that the skin had scarred, so her father created some artwork for her and covered it up.

Toni's gaze scanned the hall and then focused. He shouted at someone and in a blur of activity several nurses arrived and ushered her into a florescent room. Several coats of ointment and one bandage later, Dani's burns no longer stung.

"Let me see," he said when she emerged, slowly inspecting their work as if he would make them do it over if he wasn't pleased. He nodded his approval. Toni walked to the other end of the hall and made a call. Dani did the same. Her mother picked up on the third ring.

"You know how I feel about worry lines, Danica."

"I'm sorry, Mother." She explained the events of the night.

"Well, I know how you feel about Marcello. Is he going to be all right?"

"I'm not sure, he hasn't woken up yet. But he's stable."

"And who is this man who helped you?"

"Toni, Marcello's nephew. He's part owner."

"And?"

"And what?"

"Is he cute?"

From the corner of her eye Dani watched Toni slide his phone in his pocket and walk back down the hall toward Marcello's room. He looked pale and his broad shoulders slumped with fatigue. He fought a yawn and rubbed at his jawline, disturbing his perfectly lined beard.

His long legs carried him gracefully and his muscular thighs stretched at the fabric as he walked back and disappeared through the hospital room door. She recalled that he had to have his suits customized to fit his length. He'd need a custom bed, she thought, briefly recalling his naked form tangled in white sheets.

"Are you still there?"

"Sorry, yes."

"Well? Is he?"

Suddenly the door to the room opened and Toni jerked his head toward the inside. His wide smile touched the light in his eyes. *He's beautiful*, she thought. Maybe too beautiful for a woman like her.

"Umm…he's okay. Look I have to go, I think Marcello is awake. I'll see you later."

"I hope so, but I'm leaving for hair and makeup after lunch. The Chanel show is at 7 p.m., Danica. Wear something fabulous. If I don't see you before then I'll leave your pass on the table."

"Okay. I love—" She heard the click and sighed, then walked back to Marcello's room.

Marcello's eyes were slits under bushy white brows and his voice was more gravelly than usual, but the grip the old man had on Toni's hand was strong. He'll be okay, Toni thought-wished.

"Do you remember what happened?" Toni half whispered, careful not to wake Sophia.

Marcello nodded, gesturing for water, which Toni poured quickly and handed to him. "The restaurant," Marcello said after a few sips from his paper cup. "What happened?"

"We took care of it, but I don't think you should worry about this now."

"Who cooked?" Marcello barked, color coming back to his cheeks.

"Gianni walked out, so your old friend Danica stepped in."

Marcello smiled like a proud father. "How was she?"

"She's a remarkable chef. A bit stubborn. Too precise when it comes to plating. Obviously the dishes had an American twist to them, but overall it was successful."

"Wow, I feel like I just got graded by a substitute teacher," Dani said behind him, flashing Toni a dark look. "Marcello," Dani whispered with tears in her eyes. "I'm so glad you're awake."

Toni stepped back as Dani and Marcello embraced and Toni caught a tear in Marcello's eye, as well. Because he had no children of his own, Marcello had spoiled Toni rotten. He had the feeling he'd done the same to Dani too.

"Let me see your hands," Marcello asked Dani. Marcello always said burns were his badges. A real chef had scars. Marcello inspected the marks on her hands, then pulled her fingers to his lips for a fatherly kiss. "Now, tell me, what did you make last night?"

Letting them catch up, Toni sat down and put a hand on his sleeping daughter. He looked forward to the day they could talk like Marcello and Dani were, instead of this constant push-pull of rules and values.

"Toni thought the Nebbiolo was the best choice for the dish," Toni overheard Dani say, "but I thought the Sangiovese was a better choice."

"The Nebbiolo was a 2010 from Asti, Marcello. Perfectly balanced. They loved the wine."

Dani whipped around as if she was surprised he was listening. "Sure, it was a nice wine, but it was so rich it overpowered the shiitake mushrooms."

"It was perfect with the spiced lamb, Danica."

"I wouldn't call it perfect. It was too full-bodied."

"Since when is a full body a bad thing?"

Her head whipped around again and he suppressed a teasing smile. He shouldn't have said that but it just came out.

Dani's gaze was steady on his, probably debating if he meant what she knew he meant. Her lids narrowed slightly as she mentally debated a response. She wore her temper on her face. It was adorable, Toni thought. He held his breath at her reaction, but the mood was undercut by a rumbling that turned into loud laughter.

"You two," Marcello sighed. "I can only imagine what it looked like in that kitchen." The old man slapped his thigh and Dani pursed her lips at Toni before giving him her back. "You both have a point, but I would have gone with the Dolcetto. Big enough for the lamb, but light enough to allow the mushrooms their flavor."

Both Dani and Toni opened their mouths then closed them. He smirked at the side-eye she gave him over her shoulder.

He'd meant what he'd said about their meeting feeling like fate. And each time he felt drawn to her; an unfamiliar feeling since his divorce. He shook his head as he recalled the phone conversation he'd had with Ava that morning. On and on about her night out, not one inquiry into Sophia or Marcello until he brought it up.

He couldn't understand how he had fallen so hard for a woman who was clearly selfish and narcissistic. The only explanation was that he had been selfish and narcissistic too. Once Sophia was born, he'd changed, but he still wasn't sure he could trust himself and his feelings when it came to women.

Which made it even more difficult to achieve his ultimate goal of having a stable family for Sophia. Marry a woman who was a good role model for Sophia. Love could be learned, right? It didn't always have to be the tractor pull of desire. That had proven to be a trap.

Dani's full laugh broke his train of thought. She was still wearing her dress from last night, which sparkled in places under the bright lights. He wondered how she managed to still look beautiful after a night on her feet and a few hours of sleep in a hospital room.

"You're staring at her." Sophia uncurled from an awkward fetal position and piled her hair on top of her head.

"I am not," Toni said back, pulling her in for a kiss on her head. Maybe he was.

A nurse and doctor entered the room and shooed them out while they performed an examination.

"He seems good," Dani said to Toni.

"Let's hope the doctor thinks so. I need to get Sophia home. I just want to talk to the doctor first. I can drop you off at your hotel too."

"Thank you." Dani nodded.

"First we need some coffee."

Toni arrived with espresso and pastries just as the doctor came out of the room. The doctor took her glasses off and pulled Toni to the side.

"Your uncle suffered a mild heart attack. We found some calcified arteries around the heart and one of his valves gave out because of it."

"What does that mean?"

"His heart is working overtime. This was a warning."

Toni frowned at the doctor's serious tone. "I understand your uncle is a chef and spends hours on his feet. If he doesn't have surgery to unblock those arteries, he won't be able to continue without the threat of something far worse."

Toni tried to wrap his head around the fact that Marcello may not be able to run the kitchen any longer, or possibly die.

This wasn't good.

"Okay, so what happens now?"

"He needs rest. We are keeping him for a few weeks for observation and depending on how he wants to proceed with treatment, maybe longer. If you need to discuss anything with me please call during my office hours." The doctor turned and entered another room.

Toni's gaze shifted to Dani and Sophia, who both were staring pointedly at him.

"He's okay. But he needs to stay here awhile."

"What about the restaurant?" Sophia asked.

"Nonna can take care of it."

"I mean the other one." Toni looked gravely at Sophia.

Dani turned and looked between the two of them. "What other one?"

They filed back into Marcello's room and Toni grabbed Marcello's hand. "We can postpone the opening. You need to get healthy. With Mamma running Via Carciofo we have no one in the kitchen and—"

"No, I am getting out of this bed. I feel fine."

"That's not the doctor's orders."

"I don't take orders, young man, I give them." Marcello rolled up to sit, then clutched his chest as pain showed on his face.

Dani flew to his side. "Lie back, that's an order. Now. What's going on?"

"We are opening a new farm-to-table experience next week a few miles outside of Milan on our family villa," Toni said.

"It's taken over ten years to build," Marcello continued. "The garden is fully grown and the vineyard is now producing enough for wine making."

"A vineyard?" Dani asked.

"Toni has been growing wine grapes and selling them to wineries for years. We finally got him to start producing wine. They are excellent."

"Let me guess. No menus."

"No menu. And only produce from the farm. The rest is sourced locally."

"Wow. You've been talking about a country restaurant since I've known you."

"That's why I am getting out of this bed."

"Uncle, you could die." The room stilled at Toni's truth.

Dani took Marcello's hand when the old man's bottom lip quivered. "Postpone it. It took ten years, what's a few more weeks?"

"Yes, we'll contact—" Toni started, but Marcello cut him off.

"No! Invitations have been sent. Ryan White sent me a personal email and said he was coming. Ryan White!"

Dani sighed, the food critic for *The Taste* had a blog that could make or break a restaurant.

"Dani can run it," Marcello said into her eyes.

"What? No, I can't…"

"You handled it last night. Toni said you were amazing."

Dani glanced at Toni, whose gaze hit the floor.

"I'm not going to be here that long."

"You have an open-ended ticket."

"Because my mother doesn't know where she is going

after this. I'm not you…" Dani took a deep breath and said it aloud. "I'm a ghost chef."

"You are more than that."

"No, I'm not."

"I agree with Dani. She shouldn't do this," Toni said behind her.

Dani's mouth dropped. What the hell? Shouldn't he be begging her to do this?

"We invited a ton of press," Toni said to Marcello, avoiding Dani's eyes. "I'm not sure having her there would attract the type of press we want."

"Antonio Lorenzetti you are out of line!"

"Please, sir. I mean no disrespect, but we have sunk too much time and money to have negative press attached to this project from the start."

Dani rose from Marcello's side. "Excuse me? But what the hell are you talking about? I ran a two-Michelin-star kitchen!"

Toni's mouth was a thin line. He pulled out his phone and held up a familiar blog. When the Chef Can't Cut It splashed across the page of *The Taste*. She began to shake before she grabbed his phone and scrolled.

Sous-chef Danica Nilsson had a meltdown…
Rumored lovers…
Andre taught her everything he knows. She was talented but missed the nuances of certain dishes. It didn't phase Andre, who delivered a fantastic chef's special of veal shank.

That was *her* chef's special!

Hate for Andre and hurt from Toni made her legs weak. She handed the phone back to him and fell into a seat. "He's right. You can't have me there," she said quietly, handing the phone to Marcello.

"I don't have my glasses," he said, waving the phone away.

"It's not good, Marcello," Toni said.

"You be quiet," he barked at Toni. Sophia chuckled, then was silenced by a look from her father.

"Dani. I don't care what that blog says. I need your help." His eyes slid to Toni. "We need your help."

Toni shook his head, his gaze locking with Dani's.

Chapter 8

It was a little after ten in the morning when Dani arrived at her hotel. She tossed her purse on the table, announced her presence for which she got no response, then stripped off her clothes, wishing she could erase the night.

Toni had said she would be bad press. It took everything she had not to lash out or, God forbid, cry. Instead, she declined Marcello's offer, kissed her mentor and Sophia, then walked out and hailed a taxi to the hotel, trying to forget the way Toni looked at her.

Because he was right. That blog had shredded the little reputation she'd had and made Andre look like a saint for allowing her to work with him. No one deserved that type of press at a restaurant opening. She was embarrassed and took solace knowing she probably wouldn't see Toni again.

Her shower was heaven and the power nap she took made her feel refreshed enough to actually look forward to her mother's Chanel show later that night. Dani found her laminated event pass on the table, along with a note.

Danica, here is your pass. Show this at the door. The show starts at 7. I tried to get you something Chanel to wear but there was no time. I hope you brought something fabulous.

Dani rolled her eyes, deciding not to be annoyed by the Chanel comment. Chanel didn't have her size, as her mother well knew. But Dani did have something fabulous and she hurried to her suitcase and pulled out the black Zac Posen tea-length evening dress to air it out. It was beauti-

ful. Black satin with long sleeves and a high neck. Dani
fingered the sleek fabric as she adjusted it on a hanger. She
had an idea to pull her hair back in a wet look like in those
Robert Palmer videos, or like Trinity in *The Matrix*. She
turned the dress around to inspect it and lost her breath. A
large discoloration was splattered across the back.

"You have got to be kidding me." After a thorough inspection of the stain and her suitcase, she found an exploded
bottle of benzoyl peroxide face cleanser laying waste to
several of her clothes. She wanted to scream. Or die. Or
both. The dress she wore to Marcello's restaurant lay in
a plastic bag and smelled like food and body odor. The
Posen was the only other dress she had brought…and it
had been expensive.

She slumped on the couch. If this were *Pretty Woman*
she could call downstairs and have someone find her a suit-
able dress, except she wasn't Julia Roberts, nor a size four.
Her gaze landed on the clock. Her idea to relax and order
room service before the show just got shot out of the water.
She picked up the phone and dialed the concierge, who was
not only appalled by her plight, but ready to drop his post at
the hotel and go shopping with her. David, her new bestie,
practically pulled her by the elbow to Via Montenapoleone.
Dani hadn't done much designer shopping as a poor young
sous-chef, but the Quadrilatero d'Oro or "rectangle of gold"
was famous for its haute couture and Montenapoleone was
one of its most famous streets.

They passed by Dior, Louis Vuitton and Prada before
slowing in front of a posh-looking boutique. The glass ex-
terior revealed well-dressed mannequins, racks of sparkling pieces along the back wall and a staircase to a second
floor of shoes.

David embraced a tall man in an impeccable suit who

was smoking outside. He threw the lit bud to the concrete when he saw Dani.

"Miss Nilsson. Welcome. Welcome! David said you have an emergency. I'm Fredrick, at your service. *Sei davvero bravo!*" Fredrick yelled to David, who took off before Dani knew what was happening.

"Um, hello, I need—"

"A dress. I know. I have several already racked. Come, come."

"But…" How did she put this. "I kinda just wanted to walk around a bit and see if anything strikes me."

Fredrick looked her up and down. "Madonna, with all do respect. Many don't carry larger sizes. I, however, do. And these dresses are *magnifico*. You will look incredible, I can already tell."

Flattered, Dani followed Fredrick inside, then frowned when he locked the door behind them.

"You usually lock the door?"

"We aren't usually open during lunchtime, but I made an exception for David. Fashion emergencies are the best kind. Now—" Fredrick grabbed the sparkly dress rack and wheeled it her way. He held up a strapless gold lamé mermaid dress. "Let's get started."

An hour later she had gotten through only half the rack.

She stood in front of a full-length mirror in an eggplant-colored sleeveless cocktail dress with a plunging halter neckline and no back.

"Yes!" Fredrick shouted.

"No," Dani said back.

"Let your hair down," commanded the shopkeeper. She had put it up for the last dress, now it was coming down again. She remembered why she barely shopped, it was exhausting. Curling waves hit her shoulders. "Yes!"

"I'm naked, Fredrick."

"We'll put gold shimmer lotion on your skin…" He clapped his hands.

She shook her head and tugged on the neckline, which was showing too much side boob. "My breasts are out!"

"Of course. That's the style. They look fabulous! If I had a bosom like this I would show them to the world. The world must see this bosom."

Dani looked at herself. She could just see herself tripping and executing a Janet Jackson nip slip. Suddenly she envisioned Toni looking at her, his hand sliding inside the fabric to her naked breast. This was a "fuck me" dress, and after what happened that morning, that was never happening again. You know what else was never happening? Letting a man dictate her career. She needed to talk to Marcello again.

"I don't think so, Fredrick. Next dress. We have to hurry, I have one more stop to make."

Finally, she found a dress, received a much-needed pep talk from Marcello at the hospital, and got ready at the hotel, making it to the show just in time. The venue was buzzing with editors, photographers, bloggers and celebrities; all were talking one second and posing for a selfie the next. Dani flashed her pass and took her seat smack in the middle of the auditorium and only three rows from the stage. She ran a hand over her loose curling hair and adjusted her dress, a purple satin halter with a plunging neckline and gold heels. Fredrick had her so gassed she fell in love with the dress, but now, surrounded by the glitterati, she felt out of place.

The back of Anna Wintour's famous bob was down and to the left, while André Leon Talley's fur-clad shoulders were blocking everyone behind him to her right. For a second the lights dimmed and camera phone flashes burst through the dark like exploding stars. Then the stage exploded in music and a warm glow as young Amazon women began to prance down the runway like Thoroughbreds.

Dani couldn't get over how sleek the models were. No Photoshop or flattering camera angles. These women were slim goddesses. A woman in front of her held her camera in the air for video as a stunning blonde emerged in a gown. The crowd roared and chatter around her was peppered with "she looks great" and "she's still got it." Dani couldn't place the model, but in seconds it didn't matter. The music changed and her mother appeared on the stage.

Francesca's slower, stately walk created elegant movement in the gold taffeta and leather-corseted gown she wore. Her skin glistened with baby oil and she wore a pink wig piled high on her head. Marie Antoinette meets Grace Jones?

"Damn, I hope I look like that when I'm old," someone whispered.

"You wished you looked like that now," another said. "Is she really fifty?"

André Leon Talley threw a props snap in the air.

Her mother walked amid cheers and applause several times during the show, and by the end, Dani felt pride for her mother. They didn't always see eye to eye, and Francesca would never win a Mother of the Year award, but her mother never gave up on her dreams or her career, and for that she was inspiring. Dani had a dream of running her own kitchen and she'd made a decision earlier that day that would get her closer to that dream. Marcello had always told her that the best chefs pushed the limits. So that was what she was going to do.

Dani made her way backstage, weaving between tripods and news anchors praying the side of her face wasn't showing up in the background of interviews and photos.

Models were half-naked, changing anywhere they could find a spot and vloggers were talking into their phones. She found her mother still in the last outfit she walked in, surrounded by industry people.

Dani recognized an older and slimmer Roberto, her mother's make-up artist and dearest friend, buzzing silently around her mother with makeup brushes. A pat of powder here, a spritz there. Feeling like an eight-year-old again, Dani turned back toward the throng of people with the intention of texting her mother and heading back to their hotel.

"Daaanicaaa!" Roberto came toward her with his arms stretched wide. His hug was hot and sweaty, but welcome. It had been a long time. "Let me look at you!" He gave her a dramatic once-over. *"Belissima."*

Dani smiled a thank-you and tried to hide how uncomfortable she felt standing in the throng of size zeros.

"She did well tonight, Right?" Dani said.

"Oh! It was like 1985 all over again. She is fierce on that stage, like a panther." Roberto bared his teeth and clawed the air. Dani smothered a laugh.

"Well, she looks busy with press. Can you tell her I'm heading back to the hotel? And that I'm really proud of her?"

"No. No. No. Mommy dearest said you have to come to the after party." He handed her another pass. "Then you can tell her how proud you are yourself. *Addio, bella.*" He clapped his hands and kissed her cheek before disappearing through the crowd.

After party? The address on the card said the Armani Ristorante. There were three restaurants Dani loved to visit when she was in Milan and the Armani was one of them. She wondered if Martin still managed the place and felt her heart flutter. Martin had been a line cook and her first real boyfriend. She thought about their goodbye kiss years ago and then wondered if a taxi would be the quickest way there.

Where the hell was she? Toni prowled round the bar at the Armani Ritsorante and downed his second complimentary champagne. Sliding by a server, he switched out his empty flute with a full one and took another swig.

Ava's call took him by surprise. She wanted to talk… about what? And why here in this crowded space? He plucked a few crudités from the buffet table and blew out a frustrated breath. She had a way of manipulating him that he didn't see coming until after the fact, like tonight. He'd agreed only to talk, the next thing you knew he was arranging a babysitter for Sophia and going to the show. Watching her walk the show had brought back memories, good and bad. As did the Armani. Maybe that's why he was in a mood. The back couches were where they had gotten engaged.

A woman approached with a smile and an inviting gaze that ran down his body. He nodded politely, uninterested but conscious of offending the lady, and turned away. Dark eyes, generous hips and a floral tattoo had been haunting him all day. As did the look on her face when he protested her working at the restaurant. It wasn't his finest moment and all he could think of was begging her forgiveness, then making passionate love to her.

Toni chatted with the few people he knew by association, then sank into a couch in the back corner. He texted Sophia, who was at home with a babysitter, and smiled at the poo emoji she sent him. Because of the other night, he had vetoed her plans to go to the movies with her friends. They had yet to have their family talk, but the person he really needed to talk to was Ava. She needed a reminder that family was the most important thing in life. Not this charade, he thought, scanning the room of drunk fashionable people.

Speaking of which, he spied his ex-wife making her way through the crowd toward him. Her silver dress was as thin as tissue paper and hugged the slender contours of her body. Only a dead man would be able to look way, and yet the vision in front of him was blurred by years of painful baggage. He rose when she reached him and executed kisses on both of her cheeks. He was taken aback when her mouth slid to the corner of his on the last kiss.

Ava sat on the leather chair across from him and they exchanged pleasantries, with him congratulating her on the show, and her going into detail of the backstage antics. He sipped his champagne and nodded at the fluctuations of her voice. She hadn't mentioned leaving Sophia home alone, or the text he had sent, to which she had never replied. As usual, she hadn't inquired into his life, something he hadn't realized until after they'd married.

As she spoke, his gaze shifted as another barrage of people entered the bar and he glimpsed a shining cascade of black curly hair moving tentatively through the throng. Danica? She wore a purple satin dress that showed lots of skin and hugged her soft womanly curves. The tattoo on her arm looked like a wild accessory. He blinked as she wet her red lips and leaned over the bar to speak to the bartender.

"Are you listening to me?" Ava frowned.

Toni shifted his gaze back to his ex. He hadn't been, but answered with a confident, "Of course."

"Well, would you like to?"

Oh God, what was she saying? "I don't know…" *What you are talking about?*

"I think family dinners on Sunday would be nice for Sophia."

"Oh! I mean…you're right I think I can make it work."

He frowned as she stood and moved to sit next to him. "And then we can work on us too."

Suddenly the air in the space got thin. He took a gulp of champagne as she slid a hand on his thigh. He willed himself to relax. Ava could smell fear. And rejecting the mother of his daughter needed to be done with more finesse than a polite grin. He knew Ava, and as beautiful as she was, she was insecure. If she felt the tiniest bit rejected, she would try to hurt him by using Sophia.

He recalled how he went to court to stop her from taking Sophia to another country during their divorce. When he found out she still planned to leave, he promised her a generous monthly allowance if she stayed. He was still paying it.

Toni set down his glass and twisted toward her, taking her hand from his thigh and enclosing it in his.

"Ava, for Sophia's sake," he said as she leaned in and he dodged a kiss, "let's take this slow. We have to be sure this is what we want, no?" She tipped her face to his, her eyes glassy and unfocused. He inwardly sighed, suspecting she was on something.

"You want to be a family. So do I."

"We are a family. But you and I have history."

"History is good." Her other hand reached for his groin and he caught it and brought it to his lips.

"We need to know each other again. Let's start with the dinners," he pleaded.

"Don't you want me?" She pouted.

"You're very beautiful, Ava. Always." He was relieved at her smile. And he hoped this notion was a product of whatever drug she took, and that it would wear off along with the effects.

He let his guard down, satisfied that he had wriggled

out of a bad situation, when she grabbed the back of his head and crushed her lips against his. His first instinct was to struggle, but that wouldn't go over well. He leaned into the kiss, ran his hands over her arms and tangled his fingers in her hair, then gently cupped her jaw and pulled his lips from hers.

Ava gazed at him with a triumphant smile. He gazed back under lowered lids, hoping his eyes didn't reveal how annoyed he was. He pulled back farther and looked over Ava's head, right into Dani's eyes.

Chapter 9

The severe beige, white and black decor of the Armani Ristorante was the perfect playground for Chanel's partygoers clad in sky-high heels, glossy hair and jewel-toned lips. Inquiring about Martin at the bar, Dani held her breath when she saw a man with dark hair and swarthy skin come out from a back room and make his way toward the bar. Dani caught Martin's attention with a small wave and his face lit up as he came around the bar to stand in front of her.

"Wow. It's been too long." He leaned over so his Spanish-Italian accent was thick in her ear, cutting through the music. "Nice dress." Martin was even more handsome than Dani remembered and the way his gaze dipped into her cleavage made her blush gratefully.

His flirty smile was infectious. She smiled back, feeling at ease suddenly. He hadn't changed, which was nice considering that she was still feeling out of place in the throng of the fashion obsessed. She wasn't used to showing this much skin, even though every dress that walked by was held together by a thin strap or a barely there chain. She shook her hair over her shoulders for a little cover, but Martin swiped one side away with his hand before suggesting they grab a lounge chair to catch up.

Dani and Martin dodged servers in pastel wigs, some stopping him for a quick issue. She remembered when they had both been poor, ambitious cooks taken under Marcello's wing. Now he was the manager of a Michelin-starred restaurant. And she was…she didn't want to think about it anymore.

Toni's look when he showed her the blog said it all. His

eyes had accused her of being a fake. Meanwhile, he'd kissed her in the kitchen like a man who'd been trapped in the desert. He hadn't been calling her fake then, had he? *That kiss.* Martin caught up to her and steered her toward the back of the room, his gaze running over her bare shoulders.

Martin was going to help her forget about that kiss.

Dani scanned the lounge area and did a double take when she saw Toni kissing a lithe blonde.

"Excuse us," she said, quickly turning away. Dani sighed. Would she ever get away from this man? "Let's have a seat over here, Martin." Martin followed closely behind, then stopped.

"Toni! And Ava! You two are back together?" Dani whipped around at Martin's declaration. Did Toni know everyone in this town?

Toni stood and grasped Martin's hand like an old friend. Dani noted that the blonde didn't turn around, taking the opportunity to apply more lipstick.

"You should come find me, Toni," Martin said. "I spoke to Anton, who spoke to Destin, who said I need to speak to you—" Martin poked Toni playfully "—about the Deschamps wine."

"I was coming to you, Martin. Of course we want Deschamps here." Toni slid his gaze to Dani and she responded by putting her hands on her hips. "But you are busy right now," Toni said, gesturing toward her with a flick of his chin, "so I'll find you tomorrow afternoon."

"I'm holding you to that." Martin turned to Dani. "Dani, come meet Toni."

Dani didn't move. "We've met. *Buona sera*, Toni."

"*Buona sera*, Chef. You look lovely," Toni said, sliding his hands in his pockets.

Dani raised a brow. Chef? Was that a barb?

Martins gaze darted between the two of them. "You know each other? How?"

"Marcello."

They said simultaneously.

"Ahh yes!" Martin continued. "Dani and I knew each other when she was his sous-chef. I heard he was in the hospital. How is he doing?"

"He's well. I saw him this morning…" Toni said.

"He's better. I saw him this afternoon…" Dani said.

They both started talking and then stopped, silently competing.

Toni cleared his throat and spoke to Dani. "This is my ex-wife, Ava." Ava finally twisted around to give Dani a once-over and a half smile that didn't reach her eyes. Dani looked away, doing her best not to feel self-conscious. She recognized Ava as one of the models that walked in the show and suddenly her designer dress felt like a potato sack. Of course Toni's ex was a model. It was par for the course, right? Hot guy, hot girl. The building blocks of every perfect match. Dani cringed inside.

"Would you like to join us?" Toni suggested, looking out the side of his eye at Dani.

"No!" Ava shouted. "I mean…they seem to have some catching up to do, as do we, darling."

Dani suppressed an eye roll. "We do have some catching up to do, but *grazie*. There is room over here, Martin. *Buona sera*, Toni. Ava."

Martin and Dani settled in the open seating and jumped right into old times. Martin was as funny and engaging as she had remembered, but Dani struggled to focus on the gorgeous man that was sitting in front of her. Instead her gaze drifted repeatedly to the couple about ten feet behind him.

Dani watched Ava lean toward Toni suggestively, then

saw Toni scoot back a little. If she didn't know better, she'd say he was dodging her advances.

"And then I met Vivian." Dani's gaze slid back to Martin.

"Who is Vivian?"

"My wife."

Dani's smile flickered. Martin wore no ring and she had allowed herself to hope that he might be single. But who was she kidding? Not everyone was as pathetic as she was when it came to relationships.

"That's great. Sounds like you have it all together."

"What about you? I heard you were no longer working with Andre?"

Dani balked. "How did you hear that?"

"We are a small community, Dani. You know that."

Oh God. He'd read the blog, of course he did. "Umm... I'm exploring my options right now."

Saying it aloud to Martin made her feel like a failure, not just in her career, but in life. She saw him frown and lean in to ask more questions but over his shoulder she glimpsed her mother taking selfies with fans. She abruptly stood. "I'm sorry to cut this short, but there is my mother. Come say hi. She'd love to see you."

Dani quickly quit the couch, staring straight ahead to avoid making eye contact with Toni. She made it to the bar when she felt a hand on her arm. Whipping around, her gaze dropped to the hand, then lifted to the serious look in Toni's eyes.

"We need to talk."

"No we don't." Dani tugged her arm back and he gently released her. Her eyes flashed and he found himself intrigued by how naturally beautiful she looked in just lipstick and mascara.

"I want to apologize. It wasn't personal."

"Saying I would bring negative press is personal." She angrily flipped the heavy tresses of her hair to one shoulder exposing the plunging neckline and an expanse of skin that looked like silk.

Toni sighed. "You have to understand how much my family and I have riding on this venture. Ten years of investment is a lot of money. We won't even begin to recoup some in the first few years."

Someone shifted at the bar, allowing Toni to slip in beside Dani. Holding up two fingers, he signaled the bartender and called out something by name.

"Noted, Toni. So whom have you secured to helm your investment until Marcello takes over?"

"We spoke on the phone a few hours ago. I've suggested a few people, but Marcello has been uncooperative."

"Meaning he didn't like your choices."

Toni smiled sheepishly. "No. He didn't." They paused when two glasses of red wine appeared on the bar. "But he assured me he knows someone who will do it. He just hasn't told me who."

Toni slid a glass toward Dani and with a light swish, brought it to her nose. Toni did the same.

"Maybe he's avoiding telling you because you'll object and call them negative."

"I never said *you* were negative."

Toni watched Dani take a sip, and took his own.

"Mmm. That's very nice. What is it?"

"It's the Dolcetto Marcello was talking about." He liked her chuckle and his gaze focused on her lips when she took another sip.

She nodded slowly. "He was right. I'll have to remember this wine when I head to the villa next week. I'm staying with your mother, I believe."

Her challenging gaze caught his over the rim of her

glass. Marcello had refused to tell him who his choice was and now he knew why. His reservations still stood, but he no longer had the urge to fight her. If anything, he admitted that he was happy to know he would see her again. Toni lowered his head as if thinking, then flicked his gaze to hers. "Does it feel good to thwart me?"

"Yes. It does." She smiled.

Toni couldn't help the slow smile that spread across his face. He held up his glass and motioned for her to do the same.

"A toast to our new chef."

"Temporary chef," Dani corrected.

"What are we toasting?" Ava appeared with her hands on her hips, staring daggers at Dani. Toni felt his stomach twist. Ava was unpredictable when it came to other women.

"Dani is going to be our new chef at the villa."

Ava cocked her hip and didn't smile. "Ohhh, you're the one that took over the other night? Sophia mentioned a 'Danny.' I thought you were a man."

"No, just me."

Ava raised an eyebrow and pursed her lips, giving Dani a deliberate once-over—intimidation tactics that Toni had seen before. He had to get Ava away before she insulted Dani outright.

"It must be hard to be around all of that food, no?" Ava said with deliberate disdain.

"Ava," Toni warned. Her insinuation was subtle, but direct. Dani straightened her back and glared at Ava, but refused to engage by taking a sip of her wine.

A commanding voice came from the side.

"Well, if you ate anything, Ava, you'd know that my daughter is one of the best chefs in New York. Speaking of, Ava, have you gained a little weight?" Toni watched in awe as Francesca Watts gracefully sidled next to Dani and kissed her on both cheeks.

Ava shrank. Dani suppressed a smile. And Toni couldn't stop blinking. Daughter? His gaze darted between the two. He saw it then. The eyes and the high cheekbones were the same.

"Mother, this is Toni. I told you about him."

"Oh my." Francesca leaned in. "So you're the young man who kidnapped my daughter last night." She held out her fingers, which Toni brought to his lips. When he looked up, he caught Dani's eye roll, and then her head turned to cover it up.

"Guilty, signora. Your daughter was our savior last night."

The foursome paused briefly when a server presented a plate of mushroom and cheese croquettes.

"Ladies first," Toni offered.

"We have a photo shoot tomorrow," Francesca said just as Ava reached for a bite. A silent look passed between the two models, before Ava lowered her outstretched hand. "And Danica doesn't eat after ten."

Dani's gaze touched his, then hit the floor.

Ava huffed away.

"I'll see you at the shoot tomorrow, darling," Dani's mother called after Ava, who briefly turned with a snarl.

"Are you coming?" Ava snapped at Toni.

"In un minuto," Toni nodded, relieved when Ava sat with a group at a table.

"Odd girl," Francesca said.

"Mother," Dani warned. "That's Toni's ex-wife."

Toni almost chuckled at the questioning look on Francesca's face. It reminded him of how his own mother had looked the day he'd announced they were engaged.

"Well, I can't talk. You haven't lived your life if you haven't made a dozen mistakes."

"Oh my God, Mother."

Toni laughed. "It's all right. I find the frankness refreshing."

Francesca winked and touched Toni's arm in apology. "Forgive my American charm. And how is Marcello? The poor dear. I sent flowers to the hospital, the least I could do for taking care of Dani while I worked all those years. He was like a second father."

"Or a first father, since Dad had gone back to Sweden."

"Oh, Danica." Francesca frowned. "Your father is a creative soul." Then she turned to Toni "They're hard to pin down, which makes then so exciting I guess."

"You should visit Marcello," Danica admonished, giving him the impression they'd spoken of the subject before.

"And if I wrap early tomorrow I will. Case closed." She turned to Toni. "Now tell me about this restaurant that will be taking up my daughter's time."

"Speaking of time," Dani interrupted, "we should go. You need your rest."

"You go. Toni and I are going to have one more drink." Mother and daughter stared each other down for a moment before Dani's gaze shifted to Toni's.

After the loaded moment passed, Dani set her empty glass on the bar. "Good night, then." With a bland smile, Dani quickly moved through the bar and quit the hotel. Toni watched, fighting the urge to go after her.

When his attention came back to Francesca, she was staring at him with a half-cocked smile and an outstretched glass of whiskey. "Now, you and I have some business to discuss."

Toni froze as she pinned him with her heavily lashed gaze. *This can't be good.*

* * *

"Who does that woman think she is?" Ava jammed the keys into the lock of her front door and stomped inside. It was after midnight, and Ava had griped about Dani's mother the entire ride home. Toni lifted his gaze to the dark second-story window of Sophia's bedroom, and then he crossed the threshold and softly closed the door behind him.

The neighbor's daughter appeared in the foyer with her things, waiting for her payment. Toni hesitated a second to see if Ava would reappear, then gave the poor girl a wad of bills. He found Ava barefoot in the kitchen with a bottle of wine in her hand banging through the cupboards.

"Shhh! Sophia's asleep." He frowned at her erratic behavior. "What are you looking for?"

"The opener."

"You're opening a bottle now? It's after midnight and you have a shoot tomorrow."

She twisted the corkscrew into the top, then tugged it out. "You sound like my mother. I just need one more drink to put me to sleep. And you, my love, are gonna have one with me."

He ignored the pet name. Toni didn't want another drink; he wanted to run screaming. Toni frowned as Ava poured them both a glass. "Did you check on Sophia?"

"No," she simply said.

Toni closed his eyes in frustration, then kicked off his shoes and quietly climbed the stairs. He softly opened his daughter's bedroom door and smiled at the chaos her sheets had gone through since she was a toddler. He headed back downstairs and found Ava lounging in the living room, her glass of wine to her lips.

"She's asleep," Toni said. Another glass was waiting on the coffee table. "I'm going to head out."

"Your drink!" she called after him.

"You drink it, Ava. I'm tired."

Toni barely opened the front door when Ava shoved herself against it, blocking his way out.

"What the hell are you doing?"

"Don't you ever think about us?" The sultry tone in her voice made alarm bells go off in his head.

"Not for a long time."

"Well, what if I told you I still loved you?"

"I'd say, what about your new boyfriend?"

"We broke up." He could have predicted that.

"I see."

She slid her body against his then and pursed her lips on his mouth. Startled, he gently closed his hands around her shoulders and peeled her body from his, and then he slowly pulled his head back and gazed into her eyes. Her cherry-red lips were soft and her small breasts teased his chest. There should have been a spark or a flutter of something he felt for her long ago. Nothing. He felt nothing. And by the darkening of her eyes, she suspected as much.

"Are you in love with that chef?"

Toni balked. "Why would you say that."

"Sophia can't stop talking about her and you couldn't leave her side all night!"

"That is ridiculous. I owe her a debt. I told you what she did for us."

"Then what is it? I heard you've been seeing that teacher at school. Is it true?"

"I saw her a few times," he said with a heavy sigh.

Ava jerked back. "Think about Sophia!" Toni didn't like rising to the anger in a woman's voice, but Ava's shrill tone always sent him over the edge.

"She is all I think about. Are you thinking about her when you are out all night with new boyfriends every six weeks?" he snapped, then regretted it instantly.

Ava burst into tears and Toni wanted to hit something.

"How did we get here?" she said in between sobs. Toni worried Sophia would come down and see her mother crying. He grabbed Ava and hugged her close.

"Please, let's talk about this when you aren't a little drunk. We are doing well raising our daughter, I don't want to ruin it."

"We could be a family again," she half whispered.

Could they? Would that be best for Sophia? Ava's glassy gaze pleaded with him, making him feel like a bad guy. He wasn't the one who was coming home drunk when Sophia was a baby. He wasn't the one who cheated.

The air between them got thinner. If she could finally change, could there be a chance?

Chapter 10

The Naviglio Grande canal at night always took Dani's breath away. Romantically lit by dim streetlights, the oldest canal in Milan attracted its share of tourists, but late night boasted more locals enjoying live music and an array of food specialties. She ignored most of the soliciting from the restaurants and shopkeepers as she strolled along the canal.

Tables overlooking the water were full of family-style dishes, carafes of wine and rounds of group laughter. Charming boutiques sold an array of goods and live music filled the air.

She had her heart set on traditional Milanese cuisine. A little shellfish, maybe some veal. The perfect after 10 p.m. meal. Maybe she would snap a picture and send it to her mother. Dani rolled her eyes as she recalled the embarrassment of her mother's declaration. It had been years since Dani had followed that suggestion by her mother's dietitian.

Because it was a load of crap. Maybe it worked for nine-to-fivers, but Dani never ate while she was working—there was no time. Family meal for the restaurant she used to work in was at 4 p.m., which meant from 6 p.m. to 2 a.m., normal dinner service and clean-up hours, she was lucky to get a coffee in her system.

Those were the days that reinforced how disappointed her mother was to have a plus-size daughter. Her mother still hadn't gotten over it.

Would Francesca be asleep by now? Or would she have seduced Toni back to her hotel room? Dani thought her mother had grown out of that whole younger men phase and moved on to aging billionaires, but she could see her mother making an exception for Toni. Why else would she stay at the party?

His suit had been tailored to perfection, emphasizing his long legs and broad shoulders. She remembered his body: tall and lean, similar to a swimmer. Not overly muscular, but strong. She felt a quiver as she remembered when he lifted her off her feet. Call it a litmus test of sorts, but she liked to know that if she fell unconscious in a burning building that her man could carry her out. She chuckled to herself, imagining him carrying her limp naked body, and then she admonished herself for entertaining Toni as her man at all.

The guy didn't want her help, which was an insult to her and her cooking. That afternoon, when she had popped into the hospital to see Marcello, she agreed to do the job, but only if Toni was absent. Her mentor hadn't been happy about that contingency, but he promised her. No Toni. She didn't need the burden of sexual attraction.

And dear God, she thought looking at the moon, please don't let Toni end up being her stepfather.

"Beautiful Madonna, please!" called an older man from a narrow restaurant with tables outside. "You must try the risotto. You will think you are eating from God's own table." The man held his hands out in a dramatic plea, but she continued on the busy path with a smile and a small shake of her head.

After a few more minutes of walking, a small white-haired man with a tanned face stood proudly in front of Il Cantinori.

"*Bella*, if you are looking for the best meal in Milan you have come to the right place." She almost rolled her eyes at the boasting, but since she had been there before, she knew it was almost true. Il Cantinori was famous among locals.

No website, no phone number, just a family run place for generations.

Dani smiled and practiced her Italian. *"Quindi hai un tavolo per me?"*

"Magnifico. The best table in the house for the signora."

The old man turned toward the restaurant front with a shout, and a strong teen came flying out with a small bistro table. Dani was startled that the teen was working this late, but then reminded herself that while he was surely in school, working hard for the family was normal. He produced a white cloth from under his arm and draped it smoothly over the metal top. Then another boy set down a bottle of water and a small glass.

The old man stood behind a chair he placed facing the canal, helped her sit, then handed her a giant menu. To his surprise she placed the menu down and began to order.

"A carafe of the house red wine. The house wine is from a family vineyard if I remember correctly. And is your wife cooking tonight?"

"Signora has been here before." He winked and bowed. "I am Piero. And my wife is always cooking. I am not even allowed in the kitchen."

"Then I'll have the *pappardelle* pasta in wild mushroom sauce, the veal shanks, the scaloppine and prosciutto in the lemon and parsley sauce, the balsamic tomatoes, and the peppers with aged parmesan, all brought out together please."

He kissed the air. "The most excellent choices, signora."

When Piero stepped away, Dani slipped her feet from her heels and watched the cargo boats float by. One of the boys brought her carafe and she sipped the fruity wine from a small crystal tumbler that she decided to find and purchase before traveling home.

Home. Where the heart is? Not in her case.

Her phone buzzed. She expected to see a text from her mother, instead it was a call from Nicole, whom she hadn't spoken to in months. Dani answered.

"Girl, I need to talk to you so badly but my phone is about to die. Give me the two-minute Brazil scoop!"

"The only scoop here is that I'm still really, really pregnant, which is stupid because it's too hot to be pregnant."

Danica laughed, knowing that her friend was just being dramatic. Nicole loved being pregnant, and her husband took an enormous amount of pleasure caring for his pregnant wife. Nicole sighed as if she was relieved to sit down.

"How is Milan?"

"How did you know?"

"Destin and Toni are on the phone right now. He mentioned something about you no longer working at the restaurant."

"Wait, Destin is gossiping with Toni right now?"

"Well…they are talking about soccer or whatever. But it came up. Destin just told me. He's worried about you too." She paused. "Are you okay? Did something happen between you and Andre?"

As quickly as she could, Dani relayed what happened. "…but seriously this call may cut out my battery is red."

"Well, okay, I just wanted to know that you were okay. Nothing matters as long as you're enjoying yourself."

"I am. Remember that restaurant on the canal I met you at years ago when you were working in Milan?"

"Il Canti—"

"—nori. Yeah, I'm stuffing my face. Mother got under my skin tonight. That's a whole other phone call."

"Well, I want to hear about it. Call me when you can. I miss you."

"I miss you too."

Dani wasn't even sure Nicole heard her as her phone

went black. She tossed it on the table and smiled to herself at her friend's concern. It was nice to know you were loved especially when you were across the world. Minutes later, an expensive-looking car sped along the other side of the canal, then stopped on a side street.

Dani's mouth dropped when Toni unfolded from the driver's side and waved in her direction. What the hell? How did he know she was here? Destin! She watched him saunter over the bridge toward her. As he got closer, she noticed his shirt collar was open to the chest and his hair looked rumpled, like he'd just left a woman's bed.

"Umm…ciao," Dani said when Toni tossed his keys on the table and whistled at one of the boys for a chair. Rapidly one brought out a chair, while the other brought another wineglass. And of course, as if on cue, a procession of her meals arrived one after the other.

"You don't eat after ten, huh?"

"Do I look like a woman who doesn't eat after ten?"

He made a display of raising his brows and looking her over. A sly half smile spread across his face as he met her gaze. "I could say something but I'll embarrass both of us."

Dani narrowed her eyes. "I can take it."

"I think you look like a woman who enjoys life's pleasures. Actually, I *know* you are. And that is a good thing."

That was not what she expected. She prayed her heart would stop beating out of her chest.

"What are you doing here?" she asked lightly.

"Destin said you were here. I was watching *calcio* in the piazza in front of the Duomo with Destin on the phone."

"Calcio?"

"Erm, 'soccer.'"

"Oh, sounds manly."

"Very manly. *Dio*, this smells *fantastico*. May I?" he asked, gesturing to the spread.

It happened then. His hands spread over her back, his lips found hers and they were deep into a kiss. He sucked at her lower lip and she rose on her toes to jam her tongue fully into his mouth. She moaned and greedily clutched at his shoulders. His hands traveled down to her ass and squeezed, then roughly pulled her against him. They both withdrew, breathless. Staring at one another as if unsure that the kiss was real.

"I'm sorry," they said in unison.

"I don't... I can't," Dani started, unable to catch her breath.

"Me, neither," Toni said, his voice filled with sex.

"Good, so that's clear." Dani nodded, masking her desire to claw his clothes off.

"Yes," Toni sighed, gripping the bridge. "Clear."

Chapter 11

They'd need markers to the restaurant, Toni mused as midafternoon traffic eased. He easily navigated the unmarked country roads that stretched a little more than twenty minutes outside the city limits of Milan toward the villa, but he'd been driving the area since he was a boy.

He tried to see the roads with fresh eyes. Maybe just a sign here and there to assure their guests they were headed in the right direction? He paused, wondering if part of the novelty of what he hoped would be the most sought after food experience in Italy could be actually finding it.

He tabled the thought for after the soft opening, for which the list of attendees was growing enormously. So was his anxiety.

In the seat next to him Dani dozed, her head lulling to the side after only ten minutes on the road. He smiled. Sophia watched a video on her phone in the back seat. Teenagers. What was he going to do when she was older and going on actual dates?

Dani stirred, her face rising briefly, only to drift slowly back to her shoulder. Her hair was in a severe ponytail, making him long for the soft waves he'd seen just a day ago. Sitting with her over red wine and good food had been one of the best dates he'd had in a very, very long time. Even if she was quick to point out it wasn't a date.

When Nicole had sent him to the canal to check on her, he'd taken the charge with no question. Dani had left the party abruptly and he felt he had some explaining to do, maybe even some apologizing, for his ex-wife's behavior. Yet he remembered Dani's cool countenance as Ava threw subtle barbs about her full figure, making him aware that Dani was clearly no stranger to the slights. He glanced at her sleeping form again, taking in her smooth skin and parted lips. He wanted to apologize. He wasn't sure why it mattered, it just did.

"Papà, how much longer?"

"Not long." Glancing in the rearview mirror, her head was bent over her phone. "Do you ever put that phone down?"

"Of course. But I'm doing homework now."

"Texting is not homework."

"I'm reading. But getting texts."

"We had a deal, Sophia. You pass your next test, then you can talk to him."

"It's not him, Papà." Her voice rose.

"It better not be."

"You have a boyfriend?" Dani stirred and twisted toward the back, her brows raising in teasing question.

Toni cringed at Sophia's blush. "No…he's just a friend."

"But you like him." Dani and Sophia smiled at each other like secret conspirators, making him uneasy, like he was seeing behind a pink curtain.

"Well…he's a year older."

"What does he look like?"

"He's tall. With black hair, like really black. And green eyes."

"Sounds handsome."

"He is." Sophia said with an unconscious hair flip.

"No, he isn't," Toni gritted out.

They both peeled into laughter.

"What's so funny?"

"Have you seen him?" Dani asked.

"Yes. He hides behind a tree when I pick Sophia up from school. He's skinny."

"Tall and skinny? Sounds familiar," Dani said with a wink to Sophia he wasn't supposed to see.

"I am not skinny. You can't compare the physique of a boy to that of a man. It's like apples and oranges."

"Oh really?" Dani said with a half smile.

"Really. That boy has no muscle tone. He needs to play a sport. Like *calcio*."

"Papà almost played professionally, so he thinks everyone should play." Sophia sighed.

"And you play beautifully, *cara mia*. I taught her everything she knows."

"Maybe you could teach her friend."

"Over my dead body," he whispered to Dani, who suppressed a smile before turning front.

"What did you say, Papà?"

"I said go back to your homework. We're almost there."

Bright green hills and measures of clear blue sky were peppered with huge stone houses and acres of wildflowers.

"This is stunning." Dani stared out of the window.

"It hasn't changed much in the years my family have lived here. The roads are better, but not by much."

"Tell me about your family. What does your father do?"

"He is in banking, but you won't meet him today. He's—"

"Grandpa is in Brazil with a whole other family," came from the back seat.

"*Cara mia*, read your phone." Toni said into the rearview. Then he turned to Dani's shocked expression.

"My parents are divorced. My father had an affair in Brazil where he traveled frequently for work. I have a half sister who is about six years younger than me."

"What! That's insane. I mean, that must have been really hard on you and your mother."

"It was, but my mother has always been supported by

her own family. She has five other brothers including Marcello. They helped us through."

"How old were you?"

"I was ten when he left."

"That must have been hard. A young boy losing his father." He only nodded. He'd been devastated.

"I bet you are a better father for it though," she said low. "It makes sense why you are so protective."

Her insight surprised him. Being a good father was the most important thing to him in the world.

"All fathers are bears. Your father was protective, no?"

"No," Dani chuckled. "My parents were never married. And they both traveled so much that I only saw him for short stints at a time. Plus, my father is a Swedish hippie. He doesn't believe in discipline."

"I'm having a hard time seeing your glamorous mother with a Swedish hippie."

"He was a fashion photographer when they met. Now he owns a tattoo parlor in Manhattan." Dani held up her colorful left forearm. "It's an odd pairing, but they do seem to love each other in a strange 'I can't ever live with you' sort of way."

"Do you have siblings?"

"No. You?"

"Just Theresa in Brazil. We're actually quite close. She is a designer and sends gifts to Sophia all the time."

Theresa. The name sounded familiar to Dani. Nicole spoke of a blonde hottie who went out with Destin. "Wait, not the Theresa who dated Destin?"

"They didn't ever date, although she tried to get him into bed numerous times."

"The blonde hottie is your sister?"

Toni laughed. "Yes, and she was heartbroken when your friend Nicole came and stole Destin's heart."

"How does your mother feel about Theresa?"

"My mother tolerates my father but she loves Theresa. We are a strange family, but we've made it work."

"Amen to that," Dani said.

"And on that note. We're here."

Villa Lorenzetti rose centuries old and majestic above them with stone walls covered in vines and wildflowers. A large greenhouse stood off to the right while a newly finished barnlike structure took over acres to the left.

"You grew up here?" Dani stared in awe. Her gaze scanned the greenery and landed on the pond surrounded by ducks several yards away. "It's like a dream."

"I went to a boarding school in the city. When school was out, I was here."

"Luca!" Before Toni could switch off the engine Sophia jumped from the back and ran toward his mother's small beagle mutt, who was running toward the car at full speed. His mother appeared from the side of the house, sliding her feet from her gardening slippers into her heeled shoes. Toni felt a rush of affection for her.

"I should probably warn you now that my mother can be…commanding."

Sophia and his mother embraced, and then she waved Sophia and the dog toward the house. Toni suspected a full meal waited for them.

"Meaning she likes things her way," Dani said.

"Exactly. But she's gentle about it."

"I think I can handle that."

He recalled his meeting of Dani's mother and imagined she could handle it.

Unlike Ava, who met his mother's suggestions and invitations with flat-out refusals. Ava never participated in picking vegetables in the garden for a family meal. She didn't want to get dirty or for the wind to muss her hair.

She refused to pet the dog or even sit in the same room with him. She complained so hard that the Wi-Fi was spotty that he spent a ridiculous amount of money rewiring the house.

And his mother had tolerated all of it for him. She was his wife, after all, and the mother of her only grandchild. Yet his mother's patience, and maybe his own, had thinned the day his mother had thrown a family baby shower for Ava and she'd refused to eat the special meal his mother had prepared. It was too heavy, Ava had complained.

Just thinking about Ava's obsession with her weight during her pregnancy made him angry. She'd gained the minimum amount and Sophia was born premature with low birth weight. Seeing his baby on a feeding tube had been a nightmare. His mother had talked him through it.

Dani wasn't Ava, but what if there was something else? What if she hated the wind or needed to watch HBO? He refused to make his mother uncomfortable in her own home gain.

He sighed and slammed the car door, making Dani turn and search his face.

"Are you okay?"

He blinked. Ava had never been in tune with his moods.

"Yes. It slipped."

Dani opened the back door and reached for her coat and her smaller bag, which was nestled next to his and Sophia's belongings.

"I'll get that—"

She held their coats and slung both bags over her shoulder.

"You get the big ones," she said with a smile. Her ponytail swung and kissed her exposed neck. He tore his gaze from the supple skin at the open neckline of her Henley before it drifted farther down to the two undone buttons at her cleavage.

His body heated, recalling how soft she felt against him by the bridge.

"Antonio! Get her bags!" His mother's voice was like a splash of cold water.

"Mamma, she doesn't listen to me. Like you."

His mother came forward with a snort of laughter. Then she held out her arms to him, holding his face and kissing him on both cheeks. She turned to Dani with open arms.

"Welcome, Danica! Welcome. I am Grace Lorenzetti. We are so excited to have you here and I get to practice my English." Dani leaned in to the kisses with a smile and Toni relaxed, aware that his anxiety was popping through at random. He needed to calm down. It wasn't like he was introducing a new girlfriend. She would be working with them. And when Marcello was well, she'd be leaving.

He adjusted the roller bags in both hands and scowled.

"Food is getting cold. Come, come."

Toni watched Dani follow his mother into the house and once he'd gotten the rest of their belongings into the hallway, he found the three of them in the kitchen.

Sophia noshed on a *pizzelle* and Dani held a full glass of wine. The kitchen island was filled with meats, cheeses, olives, herbs and fresh vegetables. Olive oil and bread acted as centerpieces beside a bouquet of wildflowers.

"It's lovely here. Marcello mentioned there was a vineyard on the property."

"It's behind the restaurant. One of the special dining rooms has a gorgeous view." His mother opened the oven and removed two long pans of lasagna. "Sophia, stop eating all of the cookies and check the pasta."

"I'll do it." Dani found a fork and dipped it into the boiling pot. Expertly she rolled the spaghetti and flicked a string into her mouth. His mother caught his gaze and wiggled her brows. He rolled his eyes back at her. It was an age-old test his mother performed on all the women he brought to the house. If they asked to help they got points. If they knew how to test the pasta, they were marriage material.

Ava had failed.

"One more minute. That lasagna smells divine."

Toni snatched a *pizzelle* from Sophia's hand and put it in his mouth. "Mamma, you cooked enough for ten people."

"You and Sophia polish off one lasagna by yourselves. Danica and I want to eat too."

Without asking, Dani reached for the strainer and tackled the pasta. "What else do you need? I see garlic. Do you need it chopped?"

"You will be doing enough cooking starting tomorrow. Sophia needs to learn how to dice properly."

"Nonna, I'm better. Dani showed me." Sophia popped up from the table and found a knife and a small garlic bulb. They all watched as she began to slice, slow at first, then with a little more fervor.

His mother let out a happy yelp and tears sprang to her eyes. She grabbed Sophia to her chest.

"Such a good girl."

"Ma, it's a little garlic."

"It's tradition. Now, Toni and Dani finish setting the table. Sophia and I will finish here."

Toni poured himself some wine.

"Follow me."

Toni stopped at the elaborate setting. The cherrywood table shined. His *nonna*'s good china and crystal goblets graced four place settings. A chilled decanter of Lambrusco sat at the head of the table. Silver utensils sat in a pile for placement.

What the hell? The last time his mother brought out the china he'd brought Ava to meet her. Alarm bells went off in his head.

He planted the wineglasses on the table and whipped around to Dani's confused look.

"I'll be right back."

"Sophia, go help Dani," he said, storming back into the kitchen. He waited till she left and lowered his voice to a whisper. "Mamma, why is the good china out?"

"Whaaat? I know it's not romantic having your mother and daughter at the table, but—"

"Romantic? What are you on about?"

"Marcello said you liked her."

"He what?"

"He said you couldn't stop talking about her when you visited last. I must say, she's not your usual type. She's a woman."

"Of course she's a woman—"

"I mean she's not a woman-child like Ava. This one has all the curves in the right places, huh? Like your mother." She winked and elbowed him, then turned back to cutting the lasagna.

Toni knew Dani's curves intimately, but he would never tell his mother that. Not because he was embarrassed. On the contrary, his mother was a modern woman, but he just wasn't sure Dani would feel comfortable and he was doing his best to keep his hands and his eyes to himself.

"I can't believe you just said that."

"I saw you looking at her body outside by the car. You like her."

They both turned when movement came from the doorway.

Dani put her palms up. "Um… I'm so sorry. Sophia spilled Toni's wine on the table. I'll just grab this cloth."

Dani avoided their gazes and quickly snagged the white cloth from the counter before leaving.

Toni sighed hard. "I can't believe this."

Toni stared at the doorway where Dani had appeared and disappeared.

"*Grazie*, Mamma."

"You're overreacting. She likes you too."

"Mamma, stop! Wait, why do you think that?"

His mother chuckled and picked up one of the lasagnas.

"A mother knows. Now bring the other plate. You need to eat something. You're too skinny."

Toni pinched the bridge of his nose and then dropped his hand when he heard a low snicker from the doorway. His mother was gone, but Dani stood laughing behind her fist.

"I've been sent to get you."

"How much did you hear?"

"If we are talking about the part where you were checking me out, then all of it."

"I wasn't—" he held up air quotes "—checking you out."

"I saw you, but it's okay. They are spectacular…"

"Oh, I remember how spectacular they are." Her blush urged him on. "But if making sure that you had a handle on the bags is checking you out, then fine. I did it."

"The bags weren't on my breasts, they were on my shoulder. You just did it again."

"Did what?"

"Looked at my breasts."

"Well, you're talking about them."

"Yes, we are talking." She circled her hand over her face. "And my eyes are up here. Ground rule number one…"

"Maybe you should take your own advice?"

"Excuse me?"

"You've been checking me out too."

"Don't be ridiculous."

"The other night. You couldn't keep your eyes out of my shirt."

"Um, maybe you should learn how to button it."

"Well, that shouldn't matter. My eyes—" he circled his face as she did "—are up here."

"You've lost it." Exasperated but smiling at the turnabout, she moved toward the lasagna.

Toni quickly picked it up and moved around her. He turned back when he reached the doorway.

"Uh, uh, uh, eyes up here." He smirked when her hands flew to her hips. She was looking. The thought made him smile.

Toni set the second lasagna on the table just as Dani entered, half smiling and shaking her head. They both took their seats.

"What, Mamma?" Toni said to his mother's cheerful expression. Her eyes darted between them.

"I'm going to get the champagne. Love is in the air!" Her arms rose toward the heavens.

"No!" Dani and Toni shouted.

"Mamma, no more wine for you."

"Mrs. Lorenzetti, I hate to be the bearer of bad news, but your son and I aren't in love. I'm only here to help Marcello and your family and then I'm going back home to… well… I'm not sure, but back to America. There's no love affair. Not even close."

His mother leaned in.

"It's because he's too thin isn't it?"

"Ma!"

"Toni, you lost weight during your divorce and never put it back on." His mother scooped the lasagna onto his plate. "Eat this right now."

"It's because of all the women he dates," Sophia said with a mouthful of lasagna.

Toni looked at his daughter. "Stay out of this. And get that phone off of the table."

"*Dio*, I hope you aren't doing that Timber, Toni."

Sophia tossed a prosciutto strip to the dog. "Tinder, Nonna."

Toni served Dani a large helping of lasagna and Caprese salad. "Ignore them. I do."

Dani laughed, then took a bite of her lasagna. The sound she made was one of pure pleasure. "Wow, this tastes even better than it smells." His mother beamed and served her another helping even though she was barely through the first.

Toni couldn't take his eyes off Dani as she closed her eyes and took another bite, slowly licking the fork clean. *"Magnifico."*

"Is there someone special in your life, Dani?"

Toni saw Dani tense. "No, not right now. But I'm not looking, either. I think it's time to reevaluate my priorities."

"Amen to that," Toni said under his breath.

"Maybe that's best, then love can overtake you when you least expect it." Her eyes darted between him and Dani.

His mother was as subtle as an elephant in a parade.

"I've always told Toni that what he likes is not what he needs. If he'd have listened, then you wouldn't have…well you know."

"Divorced," Sophia said with a mouth full of food.

Toni raised his eyebrows at the only good thing that came out of his marriage. "Enough."

His gaze shifted to Dani. She gave him a teasing smile and he was surprised at his body's urge to lean over and kiss her. He shoved his mouth full of food instead, grimacing when his mother continued giving *advice*.

"Danica, you need a man who can challenge you. It's more sexually exciting."

Toni and Sophia moaned in appalled horror. He glanced at Dani, nervous she was becoming offended by his mother's candid speech, recalling Ava's quick embarrassment every time his mother opened her mouth, but Dani laughed aloud, her brows lifted in wonderment.

"Mamma, please. Danica likes strong quiet types, like Martin, the manager at Armani Ristornante."

His mother blew a breath from her lips. "The man can do nothing without being told. You don't want that. Listen to an old woman."

"Can I try some wine?"

Three heads swiveled to Sophia. His mother, seeing it as a right of passage, poured her a little and guided her through the swish, smell and taste. It was a beautiful sight, but one Toni would rather put off for another ten years. His daughter was growing up. Boys, now wine. What was next? Tinder as his mother had brought up? At least the dating talk was over.

"Mamma, has Marcello decided on the surgery?" He needed a distraction from any more thoughts of who was and wasn't good for him. Because regardless of how much he teased his mother, he was beginning to wonder if what was good for him was sitting right next to him.

Chapter 12

Dani quietly ate as conversation flowed around her. Marcello had opted out of surgery. She made a mental note to call him. Grace had taken over the kitchen at Via Carciofo, reducing their hours to three nights a week until Marcello was well. She'd decided to stay at Toni's apartment, leaving the two of them alone a few nights during the week.

She and Toni alone? Why did the idea make her nervous?

Grace passed Sophia the last of the Caprese salad.

"So, Dani, Toni tells me you two attended the same wedding last year." Dani choked on her wine and tried not to meet Toni's gaze.

"We did. But I didn't know of the connection to Marcello then. He never spoke of family."

"That's Marcello. Work is his life. Nothing else interferes. It's a blessing and a curse."

Toni pushed his plate away and rested his elbows on the table. "I've never known him to be unhappy with his life."

His mother began stacking dirty plates. "Marcello never slowed down. Never kept up his relationships with women. And now he's in the hospital with no children of his own."

Dani stabbed at her salad, the words hitting home harder than she'd like.

"Ma, stop." Toni pulled the dirty plates from his mother's hands. "Sophia and I will clean up."

"Okay, but we need room. I've made tiramisu."

The table groaned, too full to even think of another bite. His mother chuckled.

"Fine. You'll eat it later. Dani, I'm curious what you will

think of my tiramisu. My son couldn't stop talking about the wedding cake you made for Destin."

"Yeah, Papà even tried to make it once." Sophia scrunched her face and shook her head.

Really? This was news. Dani looked at him, but he was busy trying to get Sophia to hand over her phone. Dani recalled his intent to eat that icing off her body. She absently touched her chest, as if she could still feel his lips on her skin.

He'd just gotten a divorce then and she remembered Nicole saying that he'd been acting like a man out on parole. In other words, he wasn't looking for a relationship. But she couldn't help but feel that he seemed different. Less reckless and more guarded. She wondered just how nasty the divorce had been, and based on what she witnessed the other night, what was really going on between him and his ex.

Toni's mother finished off the last of the wine. "So, Dani, I hear you worked with Andre Pierre."

Dani tensed. "Yes, for a while."

"What's he like?"

Toni was silent and she wondered if he was thinking about their conversation at the canal. It was a fair question; Andre was famous, after all.

"He's…charismatic." Toni's lips pressed together. Dani wondered if he was thinking of the internet story. "He's definitely no Marcello. That's for sure."

"Well, few are. But I wonder why he would say that? Two Michelin stars is nothing to sneeze at."

Toni cleared his throat. "No, it isn't. You must be very proud, Dani."

Dani nodded half-heartedly, wondering why his compliment felt like a dig.

"And your parents must be so proud of you too. Tell me, what does your family do?"

Dani stopped to think for a moment. Was her mother proud? Toni saw her internal struggle and stepped in.

"Dani's mother is Francesca Watts."

Grace gasped with delight. Sophia yelled for her phone back so she could Google.

"*Incredibile*, you must have had such a wonderful child-hood."

Sophia snatched her phone from her father and her thumbs flew over the screen.

"Wow. She's beautiful. Hey, there's Mamma. And—" Sophia's face changed and she put the phone down.

Toni straightened. "What's wrong?"

"Nothing."

"*Cara mia*, hand me the phone." Sophia did as she was told, then began to stammer. "She said she wasn't going to see him anymore. I thought you two were trying... I thought..." Sophia's gaze swept between Toni and Dani before she quit the table. Fast footsteps could be heard climbing a flight of stairs.

Dani stayed very still, unable to see the screen of the phone. After a few scrolls and a long pause Toni blew out a breath and went after Sophia. Grace took the phone and shook her head, then handed it to Dani.

"Oh, I don't think I should look."

"You're going to be a part of this family for a short while, you might as well know everything. In any case, your mother looks wonderful."

Dani touched the darkened screen and a picture of her mother lounging at Just Cavalli Club with Roberto popped up. Their glasses were held up in a sweet toast between old friends. A few more models sat next to her mother, includ-ing a svelte blonde on the end in a lip-lock with an older gentleman. Ava.

Dani's heart tightened, knowing what Sophia was feeling. How many times had Dani scoured the internet for her father, only to find him in pose after pose with girlfriend after girlfriend.

Dani let the phone go dark. "It's normal for her to want her parents to get back together."

Grace began to clear the table. "She's getting older, watching everything. I'm afraid that Ava's behavior is affecting her negatively."

Dani gathered the rest of the empty plates and followed Grace into the kitchen. Grace filled the sink with soapy water and let the lasagna pans soak. Grace patted the counter.

"Just sit them here, *cara*."

"I'm happy to wash them."

"No, we can do that in a little while. I want to walk you around the garden before it gets dark. Marcello hasn't finished the menu and I thought you'd want to see what ingredients we have for you to work with."

"I'd love that."

Grace led them through the mudroom and outside across the back patio toward one of the largest greenhouses Dani had ever seen. Several plotted gardens marked the way. Squash, eggplant, snap peas, to name a few. Toni's mother planted and cared for them all herself, only using the most organic resources to keep them healthy.

Sophia's raised, muffled voice came through the air.

Grace stopped, the look on her face one of anguish. "He tries so hard with her."

"He's a good father. Better than mine had been at his age."

Grace took a turn into some of the taller vegetation, caressing the leaves as she went.

"I hope I didn't embarrass you when I insinuated you and Toni should date."

"No. I understand. You're concerned about him."

"His relationship with Ava fell apart so fast. I knew they

were wrong for each other, but my Toni had always been in love with love. I don't think he ever truly saw Ava for who she really was. They were young and codependent for a long time, never leaving each other alone. Always going out. Always partying."

"Sounds like an addiction."

"Exactly. Love was a drug to them. Then Sophia came along." Grace's eyes gleamed. "The tiniest precious little being. And of course that's what opened his eyes."

"A baby sobered them up, so to speak?"

Grace nodded. "They were fine for a little while, but once Sophia was weaned things began to get strained. Ava was ready to go back to work, which was natural. But she also wanted to start partying again. Toni didn't."

"I'm surprised. Usually people slow down a bit."

"She hadn't changed. But Toni had. He hasn't once taken his role as a father lightly. She, on the other hand…oh look, buds have begun to sprout. Watch your step."

Dani stepped over the threshold into the greenhouse, her thoughts on Toni when towers of green vegetation rose in front of her.

"Wow. These are tomatoes?"

"And some herbs. All geothermal." Blooming pots lined the walls.

"How is that possible?"

"Marcello replicated techniques used in Iceland. They produce tomatoes year-round. Now so do we."

"Oh my God, they look amazing. I'd love to taste them."

"You just did. My tomato sauce comes from these tomatoes."

"Your family has built a masterpiece here."

Grace smiled. "And you are going to be a part of it."

Dani's heart almost stopped. *Just a ghost chef. Ten years in the making. A large investment for the family. The pres-*

sure began to feel enormous. How did she get here? She was supposed to be focusing on what she wanted from her life, not filling in for someone else's life. Been there, done that.

"Are you all right?" Dani felt Grace's hand on her shoulder. "You look pale."

"Maybe I had too much wine."

"I bet you're exhausted. Let's go inside."

Toni met them in the hallway. He had his hand on one of the bags when they walked in. Following his talk with Sophia, the smile he mustered was half-hearted.

"So, Dani, what did you think of our project?"

"It's amazing." Grace continued into another room and Dani touched Toni's shoulder. "Is she all right?"

"She'll be fine."

Grace appeared with a torn, handwritten book. "Marcello's menu, so to speak. You know he prefers to surprise his guests with a dish, but he always has a list of entrées prepared in case someone is uncomfortable with that concept. Oh, I just realized it's in Italian."

"That's fine. I should be able to stumble through it."

Grace turned to her son. "Toni, you can show her the kitchen tomorrow. How is Sophia?"

"Better, Mamma. Texting. Googling. Who knows."

"Ugh! Those phones. I'm going to clean up and make us all some tea."

"Let me help, Grace." Dani stepped forward but the spry woman stopped her.

"I won't have it. You'll be busy enough tomorrow. Toni will show you your room. Rest a little. You're still a bit pale."

Toni led Dani into a spacious room, propped her spinner against the wall, and plopped her carryall on the bed.

"Welcome to my old room."

Dani's gaze slid across the walls, which were riddled

with '90s-style posters of athletes, soccer plaques, medals and a few magazine tears of models.

"Wow. I feel like I'm in 1995."

He chuckled and pulled open the curtains, exposing a gorgeous view of the garden and the small patch of vineyard further beyond.

"My mother refuses to change it. Sophia stays here when we don't have company." He gestured toward the full-size floor mirror with stickers all around the edge. "The awards on the desk are hers. Up until a year ago, Sophia played *calcio*, er, soccer, for a top club."

Dani crossed to the corner desk and picked up one of five gold statues. Her name and 1st Place was etched on the plaque. Pictures of her in uniform from past to present were displayed on the wall. She leaned closer to an action shot that could have been taken by a professional.

"Why did she stop?"

Toni shrugged and his mouth became a flat line. "She said she no longer liked the game." He turned back to the window and stared at the purple and yellow streaked sky. "We used to play a lot together, but I guess she's growing up. Becoming a young woman."

"Women play sports."

He turned back to her and smirked at her belligerent tone. "Yes, they do. But she was no longer interested, so I let her quit. And her mother never approved of her playing, anyway."

"But she was good. Am I right?"

His smile was nostalgic. "She was good."

"Was she better than you?"

"Of course not."

Dani laughed at his matter-of-fact tone.

Toni slid his hands on his pockets and sat on the edge of a small desk. "Did you play sports?"

Dani chuffed. "Does this look like the body of an athlete."

"You're strong. I can see you playing, uh, baseball?"

"Baseball?" Dani laughed in shock.

"Yeah, like, um, who's the famous guy... Babe Ruth."

Dani rolled her eyes. Of course he picked the fat player.

"No. No sports. I traveled a lot with my mother, which took me out of school three to four times a year."

Thinking back on grade school always made her cringe. Tutors, summer school, her father even tried homeschooling her himself at one point. What a disaster. Her grades were always passable, but she was lucky all she'd ever wanted to do was cook, because she wasn't sure academia would have been an option.

"For the record, I didn't choose Babe Ruth because he was overweight."

Dani flicked her gaze to his and felt her heart beat a bit faster. *Overweight.* She hated the term, an assumption that there was one weight for everyone.

"It doesn't matter."

"It does if I offended you. I saw the look on your face."

Ugh, she had a way of showing her feelings on her face. "I think you could have said Derek Jeter or Alex Rodriquez, that's all."

"Who are they?"

"Yankees."

"Oh! Right. I've seen them play."

"You have?"

"I go to New York a lot."

"Hmm. I've never actually been to a game."

"I think they kick you out of New York for that."

She smiled. "Yeah, they do."

He ran his gaze over her face as if he was going to say something else. He clapped his hands together.

"Well, I'll let you get settled. The bathroom is down the

hall. My mother left you towels there." He pointed to a futon against the wall. "And anything else…just ask."

"Thank you."

He shifted his weight, then headed for the door. "Sophia is staying across the hall. Mother is at the very end. And I'm downstairs in the *seminterrato*."

She frowned, then realized he meant the basement. "Got it."

He walked out the door, but seconds later Dani looked up from unzipping her bag to see Toni standing still in the doorway with his hands in his pockets.

"Sandro Botticelli believed that flesh was a symbol of health, wealth and stability. Which is why he depicted the most desirable women to have fuller figures. Even the statues all around Rome are of women with round hips and bellies—signs of femininity and fertility."

"You're making this awkward."

"Have you seen his paintings?"

"Everyone knows *The Birth of Venus*."

"He's done so much more than that."

"What does this have to do with—"

"You're not fat, Dani. I saw your face when your mother shooed away the hors d'oeuvres at the party. I'm sure she's curbed your hand many times, the same way Ava does to Sophia."

Dani looked away, trying to find her voice. All that came out was a whisper. "She shouldn't do that to her. It will scar her for life." Dani felt the tears gather in her throat and she began to count backward, hoping they wouldn't spring a well in her eyes.

"I've always been a big girl. Even at Sophia's age. It doesn't matter if you don't think I'm fat, or even if I don't think I'm fat. Society says I'm fat. Do you know how hard it was to find a dress for that party?"

"You looked stunning."

She met his gaze and the look they exchanged was infused with a strange, thickened intimacy. She felt her heart rate increase. The deep, dark attraction sent luxurious waves of arousal through her body. He was so handsome. The classic bone structure and masculine jawline was the perfect backdrop for his infectious smile, but this, his declaration, the way he was looking at her, like he could really see her, had cracked open something inside of her.

She wanted him. Maybe it was the way he was with his daughter or the unapologetic way he spoke his mind. Maybe it was this, his inclination to call her out of her emotional shell. He can see her, wrapped in all of her insecurities, and as he stood there with his steady gaze on her, all she could think about was going to bed with him. To slide her hands over his shoulders and down his powerful chest. To press her lips to his skin. Then pin him to the bed and crawl up his tall, strong body.

She swallowed hard. "I'm a grown woman, Toni. I wasn't offended by your comment. I'm fine. Everything is fine." *Please leave!*

"I'd like to show you his work sometime. It's at the museum in Berra."

"Fine. Let's do that," she quipped, biting her lip against the odd mingling of emotions. She wanted him; she wanted to run. *Out. Out. Out!*

Toni's gaze stayed on her briefly before he nodded and left. Dani rushed forward and quietly shut the door, then threw her back against the door and let tears roll down her face. She wasn't quite sure why she was crying. And she wasn't interested in exploring it. She wiped her face and sniffed herself back to rights. She ran her hands over her breasts and down her belly as if she could coax the arousal back inside its dark cave. Her breathing evened and she slumped on the bed, Toni's bed. She imagined him sleeping in it, then mentally slapped the fantasy away.

Then her gaze landed on Marcello's recipe journal. She flipped through the pages, letting the recipes push away her insecurities. But suddenly new insecurities rolled in. What if she failed? She tossed the book on the bed and walked over to the mirror. She ran a finger through the shaved edges at her temple, air-conditioning for the kitchen heat. Her palm ran over her tattoos, feeling the burn scars they covered. She then studied her fingertips, full of marks from cuts. She ran her hands over her breasts, down her middle, then over her hips. The image in the mirror didn't look like a Botticelli painting.

Chapter 13

Dani couldn't sleep. *You looked stunning.* She rolled to the side to shake off the conversation she'd had with Toni. His insight into the way she had been feeling was uncanny, and unsettling. Being vulnerable was bad enough, but vulnerable in front of Mister Confidence? No, thank you. And it wasn't like he could relate. He was tall and fit and always put together. She'd seen the way women looked at him. His mother was trying to make him fatter, not slimmer.

Venus in a half shell she was not. If only it was the 1400s.

The moon emerged from behind a cloud and shot a ray of light through the window to her nightstand where Marcello's book lay open. She sat up and let her eyes adjust to the writing on the pages. Tomorrow she'd begin testing the entrées, praying she could do them justice. Her eyes slid to her phone: 3 a.m. It was tomorrow.

Dani threw on sweatpants, zipped her hoodie over her tank top and padded barefoot down the stairs to the kitchen. She placed the book on the counter and as quietly as possible, began going through the cupboards. If Grace was anything like her brother, there would be huge jars of home-dried spices, sauces in the fridge, several cooking sherries, homemade pastas in the freezer and cuts of meat.

She found nothing. Other than the fresh herb pots lined along the wall, there wasn't a clue that the woman asleep upstairs even cooked. Dani walked back toward the mud-room and stopped when she saw a wide door to her right. It opened with a loud squeal, and Dani's jaw dropped. It was the walk-in closet of a chef's dream—a full steak locker, a full wine locker, jars of spices, pastas, canned sauces, barrels of ripe root vegetables and a giant refrigerator-freezer with every produce imaginable.

Dani turned on the burners and hit the ground running. Steak sizzled. Pasta boiled. The fish cuts luxuriated in butter. She tasted her first entrée and spit it out. Too much tarragon. Her second try was too spicy. Her third, meh. Fresh basil, truffles, a hint of dried persimmon. Gorgeous.

"Are you crazy? It's two in the morning." Dani whipped around to find Sophia in a big T-shirt and socks with her phone in hand.

"Yeah, maybe I'm a little crazy. I wanted to get a start on the menu. Did I wake you?"

"No. I just couldn't sleep. I thought I'd get some water." She shuffled to the counter and stuck her nose in the big pot. "What are you making?"

"It's a cream sauce."

"Can I have a little?"

"Of course! Take a seat."

Dani found a plate and served her a small helping.

"You're not going to eat?"

"I never eat when I'm cooking. Just tastings." Dani watched Sophia take a bite. The young girl closed her eyes and cocked her head dramatically. Then her eyes popped open.

"It's really good."

It was good to hear, but Dani wasn't yet satisfied and planned to make it again. She fetched the girl a glass of water and set it down when Sophia's phone went off. A text message from W came through saying, send me a pic. From the way the girl blushed and avoided her gaze Dani suspected it was from the boy.

"I used to code my boyfriend under bubbles. I don't know why I ever thought that was clever."

"Don't tell Papà."

"Okay. But maybe you should say good-night to W," Dani said before turning away. She did not want in the middle of that. Nor did she want to know what type of pics they were sending. She grabbed an onion and began dicing. When she looked up Sophia was next to her with a knife. Dani found her a cutting board and gave her several tomatoes. After a quick tutorial, Dani and her young sous-chef began to cook.

"Dani, have you ever sent a naked pic?"

Dani stopped dicing, she fixed her face and turned to Sophia.

"Um, I have. It was to a boyfriend whom I hadn't seen for several weeks."

"He says he misses me and wants a picture."

"Uhh, did he ask for a naked picture?"

"He wasn't specific, but…"

The girl's face said it all.

"He sent you one. Didn't he?"

"Yes."

"Sophia. You don't have to do anything you don't want to do and I advise against it. You don't know where that picture will end up. Send him a pic of the dog."

She giggled. "It's my fault. I asked him to send it."

Oh Lord. Dani's brows shot up, and then she pushed them back to neutral.

"It's none of my business."

"I didn't think he'd send it. We aren't having sex or anything."

"Whoa, I wasn't even thinking it."

"I'm not that type of girl." She frowned.

"I never thought you were."

"Papà thinks I am."

"He does not. He loves you so much. He's just trying to protect you from the big bad world."

Sophia's bottom lip trembled and Dani didn't know what to do, so she grabbed the tiramisu from the fridge and cut them both a piece. Dani coaxed Sophia to the table. They sat down and, after a loaded several seconds, Sophia shoved a piece in her mouth.

"I saw all of your trophies upstairs. Your father told me that you quit soccer. I mean *calcio*."

She shrugged. "I didn't want to play anymore."

"You don't miss it?"

Sophia shrugged with nothing else to say and Dani dropped the subject, happy that she was no longer on the verge of tears.

"Mamma and Papà fought about it a lot. I thought if I was a better daughter..."

Dani saw a tear plop into Sophia's dessert.

"You thought they wouldn't get divorced."

Another tear made it into the tiramisu and Dani grabbed her hand.

"Oh no, honey, it's not your fault. Trust me I know."

"How do you know?"

"My mother and father were never married, but we did all live together for a few years. I thought if I lost weight, then my mother wouldn't be so angry and my father would be able to tolerate her, so I starved myself for a month. No one noticed. But my mother kept complimenting me on how much weight I was losing, and then one day I passed out and woke up in the hospital."

Sophia gasped.

"My father moved out a week after I came home from the hospital and my mother blamed me and my 'stunt.'"

"That's crazy."

"My mother *is* crazy."

Sophia laughed. She finished her dessert and looked less on the verge of a breakdown.

"You should talk to your father."

Sophia grimaced. "He doesn't listen, just barks orders."

"You really like this boy, huh?"

Sophia blushed.

"You should get some sleep."

"I wanna help a little more. Cooking is fun."

Dani smiled. She thought so too.

Who the hell was up this late at night? Toni could no longer listen to the footfalls above him. He silently climbed the stairs and stopped in his tracks just beyond the entrance to the kitchen. Before him, Dani and Sophia had their heads together over small cuts of tiramisu. Not a bad idea, his mother's tiramisu was delicious. He took a step forward and stalled. Sophia wiped tears from her eyes.

A powerful need to rush forward gripped him, but he stayed when he saw Dani's hand settled over his daughter's. They exchanged soft words he couldn't hear and Sophia nodded sincerely, then smiled. After a few seconds, the two of them got up and began chopping vegetables at the kitchen counter.

Toni caught himself smiling at the pair they made. He contemplated going back to his room, content that Sophia was smiling again, unlike during their talk when she confessed that Ava had told their daughter they were getting back together.

He blamed himself, afraid that his promise to "think about it" had somehow led Ava to believe their reconciliation was actually happening. But he knew better than that. Ava was using their daughter as a pawn to trap him. It wasn't the first time. But, dammit, he needed to make sure it was the last.

Sophia's giggles broke into his thoughts. Dani wouldn't act like that. He shook his head, admonishing himself for the comparison. He wasn't on the market for another woman in his life, and yet he couldn't take his eyes from the scene in front of him. He'd be lying if he said his conversation with Dani hadn't been part of the reason why he couldn't sleep. The sadness in her eyes had made him want to hold her.

He motioned to slide his hands into his pockets, clenching his fists when he found he had none in his pajama pants. Something had shifted when they had been in that room together. She had looked at him with those sad, dark eyes, her body framed by his extra-large bed, and all he could think about was picking her up and pinning her underneath him. His lips at her throat and the swells of her breasts. His hands smoothing over her belly and down over her thighs.

"You can come out, Papà."

Dio. Now he looked like a Peeping Tom. A resigned smile on his face, he stepped out of the shadows and stopped just over the threshold of the kitchen.

"I was just seeing what all the noise was."

"You were lurking." Sophia popped something in her mouth.

"No, I was going back to bed."

Dani zipped up her sweatshirt before turning around. The action bothered him, like she was putting up another barrier over herself and her body. Dani gave him a weak smile.

"Sorry, Toni, this is my fault. Did we wake you?"

Toni mentally grimaced at her terry cloth armor that zipped to her neck. "No, I was awake, but I thought animals had broken in. What are you two doing?"

Sophia dipped her spoon in a pot and stirred. "We're cooking Uncle's entrées."

Dani flipped off a burner. "I couldn't sleep so I decided to practice a few dishes. Do you think your mother will be mad? I'm going to clean everything."

Toni held up a palm and came toward them, the smells making his stomach rumble. "She won't care. But you—" he pulled his daughter close for a kiss on the head "—bed. Now."

Vibrations came from the table and Toni turned to see Sophia's phone lighting up. Father and daughter lunged for the phone, but Sophia snatched it first and held it to her breast.

"Give it to me."

"No, please. I'll turn it off."

"You said that earlier and you haven't done it. Is that who I think it is?"

Sophia's gaze shifted to Dani, who quickly turned away and began stirring a large pot. "I won't answer him."

"The deal is off."

"No!" She quickly deleted the texts, turned off her phone and held it up for him to see. "It's off."

"Give it to me."

"No!"

"Now."

She slapped it into his hand and ran out of the room. He hung his head for a moment, then tossed the offending technology on the dinner table. He tugged at the collar of his T-shirt, wondering if his frustration was making his temperature rise or if it was the heat from the kitchen. Half turning, he stared into the hallway, unsure how to mend the volatile relationship he and his child were having lately. Dani continued to cook.

"She's having sex with that boy," he said to Dani's back.

"No, she's not." His head whipped up to see Dani handing him a small plate of *cavatelli* and a fork. He pulled out a chair and settled his plate in front of him.

"How do you know?" Without taking his eyes from her, he speared the pasta and popped it absently in his mouth.

His brain stopped, the garlic sauce was laced with saffron and basil, and left an aftertaste so subtle he couldn't put his finger on the spice. He forked more into his mouth and almost moaned.

"She told me just now. She's a good girl, Toni, she's just feeling a little off balance. And she's in puppy love, or whatever you want to call new love."

"She told you all of this just now?" His mood lifted dramatically. His baby wasn't having sex yet. He'd do cartwheels if he could. He'd— After another bite of Dani's heaven, Toni's mind ran toward the perfect wine pairing. He jumped up.

"Yes. She— Where are you going?"

Toni whipped open his mother's pantry and pulled out a black wine bottle, gathered two glasses and set them on the table.

"Taste this." He popped the bottle and poured with gusto.

"It's 4 a.m."

"Yeah, and you're cooking a seven-course meal. Taste it."

Her lips pursed but she acquiesced. Giving it a swish and sticking her nose in the glass before taking a sip. He smiled when her brows went up.

"Now try it with the *cavatelli.*"

He watched her take careful bites and sips. She sat back and rolled her tongue over her teeth.

"I like it. Is it a Barbera?"

"No, a Montepulciano."

"Whose?"

"Mine."

She took another sip. "No, I mean, whose vineyard?"

"Mine. It's the family wine."

"Well… I hope it's showing up on the menu."

"Alongside Marcello's *cavatelli,*" Toni said.

"Oh…this isn't on the menu. It's my recipe. I was just playing around."

Toni blinked. "I like how you play. It's going on the menu."

Dani looked stricken and shook her head. "I think Marcello has a better dish in his book, I'm just getting started really. I'm sure there won't be room for it."

Toni blinked, unable to figure out what had just happened. They'd been on the same page for a moment, and then it was as if someone had dumped cold water on them both.

"I should clean up." Dani grabbed her wine and crossed to the counter, scraping what was edible into bowls and tossing scraps into the garbage. Toni finished off the few bites of his plate, then began to run water into the sink. "I can do it."

"No, the cook doesn't clean."

Their gazes locked for a moment and Toni wondered at the sadness that seemed to have touched her eyes again. Dani broke their staring contest to hand him a plate and he noticed a small bit of sauce on her bosom.

"You have something here." She looked down at her sweatshirt and he swiped at the glob with his finger, pulling it back so she could see.

"I should have used an apron. Here."

She held out a towel, but he refused it, licking the sauce from his finger. Her dark eyes settled on his lips, then ran up to meet his eyes.

Toni stepped forward and slid his hand around the back of her neck. Before she had time to question what he was doing, his lowered his mouth and kissed her full on the lips. He wasn't prepared for the electric heat that burned through him. Her lips were soft and warm, his mouth moving over hers in a slow thorough exploration. He shifted and brought them closer, needing to feel her body against his.

Her hand moved from his neck to his cheek and he felt

the warmth of her palm as she cupped his face and kissed him back. Flashbacks of Brazil urged him on. He should have pulled away, but he could no longer hold himself back. Ground rules be damned.

He dragged her against him and plundered her mouth as if her kiss was an antidote he needed to survive. He was vaguely aware that his daughter and mother were upstairs, but his whole world came down to her mouth, the jagged rhythm of his heart and the slow, relentless pumping of his blood.

Toni continued to kiss Dani as he unzipped the offending sweatshirt and cupped her breasts through her tank top. Her moan was wild and needy, sending his brain into a fuzzy state of single-minded awareness. He needed to hear her moan again and his brain handled the logistics.

A flight of stairs to his bedroom or steps to the pantry?

Chapter 14

Dani squealed when Toni snaked an arm around her and picked her up off her feet, spiriting them both into the dark closet full of food and wine. He kissed away her questions, pressed her against the shelving, found the waist of her sweatpants and slid two fingers inside of her panties.

"I remember how you wrapped your legs around me in the pantry at the wedding," he murmured against her ear. "How you spread them wide for me on my bed. How slick you were when I was inside of you."

He groaned when he found her wet and ready for him. He made gentle, torturous circles over her swollen flesh, then slipped his fingers inside her. He closed his eyes against the warmth, and the urge to flip her around and drive himself endlessly into her sweet body.

"I want to see you come again, Dani."

She gasped and clawed at his shoulders, her hips rocking into his hand in answer.

A muffled sound intruded into his sensual haze. He paused, his ear cocked toward the door. Their breaths mingled and their eyes searched each other's shadowed expressions. Seconds went by with no further suspicion. Then Dani's hand came up, closed around his wrist and set a dizzying rhythm of her own. "Don't stop," she whispered.

Their mouths met in a hard, feverish kiss. And Toni found himself further set on his goal to facilitate her pleasure.

"Toni? Are you in here?" Toni froze. His mother's voice boomed in the room next door.

While he was aware of the sensitive situation, his feelings were feverishly impenetrable. He'd felt the first tremors of the unequivocal passion that was ready to roll through Dani's body, and he wasn't interested in stopping. Toni felt rather than heard Dani's soft gasp of alarm and, checking that the door was closed, tightened his arm around her. His fingers quickened their pace and he bent his head next to her ear and breathed, "Come for me."

Dani closed her eyes as her body shook with internal thunder. She was white-hot and panting, her fingers digging into his back and her body opening further for him. He covered her mouth to taste her pleasure, taking her breath into his body along with her muffled cries.

Seconds later another call. "Toni, are you in there?"

"Oh my God," Dani whispered in the dark, the warmth of her body shifting away from him. No, he wasn't having it. After a deep steadying inhale, he answered in a calm, controlled voice, "I'll be right there, Mamma."

Dani was shaking, racked still by her orgasm, and rigid with the possibility of being caught.

Toni adjusted his pants, then gave her a measured look before he kissed her. "Don't move. This isn't over."

Toni slipped through the pantry door and found his mother in her robe drinking a glass of water.

"Are you cooking?" She frowned, automatically reaching for the soap and sponge.

"Sophia couldn't sleep so I made her a little something. I'll clean up. You should go back to bed." Toni grabbed the sponge from her hand and walked her to the foot of the stairs.

"*Va bene*, but don't be too loud or you'll wake Danica." Grace pulled herself onto the first step, then turned and put her palm against his cheek. "You need a strong woman, *figlio*."

"You may be right, Mamma." Toni took his mother's hand from his face and kissed her fingers. There was no question of whom she was talking about, but he wasn't in the mood for a pep talk. The subject of their silent understanding was waiting for his return, and he was eager to be received.

His mother's ascent of the stairs felt like an eternity and when he heard her bedroom door shut then lock, he flew across the room and slipped inside the pantry door. He closed the door behind him and tuned on the single overhead light. His heart dropped when he saw no sign of her, but he calmed when she peeked her head up from a crouched position behind the freezer.

Dani came out from her concealed space then, her clothes righted and zipped, her eyes wide with doubt.

"She's gone," he said, his feet moving toward her on autopilot.

"Oh my God. That was close. We shouldn't—" Toni took her face and kissed her, silencing her before she could voice her change of heart. He slid his tongue against her and brought all his skill into play, hoping her change of heart would melt away just as his intention to not get involved with a woman cracked every time he saw her.

Toni lifted his lips just above hers, pleased when she held her face tipped toward him. Her eyes blinked open and he palmed her cheek. "It's time for bed."

Her gaze dipped and she pulled back with a quick nod. They quietly made their way into the kitchen and down the hall toward the stairs. Toni stopped at the basement door and reached for Dani's arm as she continued to walk by toward the stairs.

"I meant *my* bed," he said low, gently pulling her toward him.

A breath went by as her gaze took in the descending wooden staircase. "I thought you meant separate beds."

He held her gaze. "I didn't."

"We had an agreement, remember? All work and no play. Maybe we should stop."

"We haven't started working yet. And I can't let you go tonight. If you won't come down here, then I'll come up there. But I'm making love to you."

"What if I said no?"

"Are you saying no?"

Her lips parted, but nothing came out.

He closed the basement door and moved toward the stairs.

"No, they'll hear," Dani said before he cleared the first step. She opened the door and disappeared into his bedroom. Excitement flared through his senses.

Dani was standing in the open doorway that led to the garden when he descended the stairs. She was bathed in the glow of a single floor lamp, gazing into the night. He turned off the light and the moonlit garden was suddenly visible. His spacious room with its king-size bed and tan leather couch was streaked with the moon's rays, and the sound of crickets were carried by a cool breeze.

"Etheral isn't it?" he said, touching his lips to the back of her neck. She nodded and turned, stepping into his arms. He could no longer hold back and brought his mouth down in an aggressive kiss. She leaned into him and wound her arms around his neck, pulling him closer. She matched his kiss and he tasted the delicious, savory flavor of her, the sweet lick of her fiery response, and the sultry erotic slide of her tongue. Lust jolted through him and she moaned into his mouth.

"Tomorrow we play by my rules."

"Tonight we play by mine." Without lifting his mouth from hers, he yanked her zipper down and shoved off her sweatshirt. Then he shoved his hands under her tank top and willed her arms up as he stripped the cotton fabric from over her head. His ears rang with her soft moan as he kissed and sucked her exposed neck, her shoulder and the creamy swells of her breasts. His palms played and teased, and he lifted the tip of her breast to his mouth. Her hands locked in his hair as her nipple hardened with the lap of his tongue.

She breathed his name when he transferred his mouth to her other breast. Her hands clutched his biceps to steady herself and her eyes were closed against the sensations. He couldn't remember when he had ever wanted anything or anyone as badly as he wanted her.

He eased her pants down over smooth legs and silken curves, feeling her tremble under the caress of his palm. His fingers skimmed the elastic of her panties, the last barrier to where he so badly wanted to be, and he whisked them down and off. She stood before him naked; a Botticelli come to life. Finally, she was here. His.

"You're beautiful." More words were threatening to tumble from his mouth. Words of want and desire. Words of longing and obsession. Words of love. He clamped his mouth shut.

Cupping her face in his hands, he found her mouth again and drank her in, deepening the connection until his body was screaming. He felt her hands tugging on his waistband and he pulled his mouth away to help her. His T-shirt and pants were off in a heartbeat. He hauled her closer and she wound around him, her skin sliding against his, pressing against his rigid erection.

He walked her back to the bed and lowered her onto the soft duvet, covered her body with his, his arms sliding under her shoulders to protect her from his full weight. Her thighs cradled him and he was poised at her apex, feeling her soft nudges, beckoning him to fill her. She whimpered and he took the sound into his mouth, silencing her with a kiss.

"We have to be quiet." She nodded, her eyes dazed, her nails digging into his back.

"Okay," she murmured against his mouth. "Please, don't stop. I need you to—"

"I know, angel. I know." He slid his hand down between their bodies and found her silky-soft and dripping. He muffled his own groan in her neck. Then he eased his hand away and reached for the front pocket of his leather dopp kit which lay open on top of the nightstand.

Condom in place, her legs wrapped tighter around him and he entered her in slow, rhythmic thrusts, testing and filling her until he could no longer hold back. He covered her mouth with his and drove himself deep. He swallowed the desperate cry that bubbled from her throat. He stilled, overwhelmed by the feel of her. Warm and tight; honey and wine. Waves of acute pleasure engulfed him.

"Toni?" He came up from the sensory overload at her whisper. Her hand was on his face, tracing his lips and jaw. Her hips urged him on and he pulled back and surged into her again, driving the breath from both of their bodies. He rocked deeper inside of her and her eyes fluttered closed until he softly ordered, *"Guardami."* "Look at me." His hand slid under her bottom, and he lifted her to meet his full, hard length.

"Oh…" she gasped, and then she slammed a hand over her mouth and stilled. They looked at each other wide-eyed and both peeled into a silent chuckle.

"I feel like I'm fifteen," Toni said, nudging her hand away from her mouth with his lips for a kiss. "But sex was never this good then."

He rotated his hips slightly to touch all of her lushness and drove home again, watching her back arch and loving the way her hands fisted in his hair. The words began to fall from his lips then. Staccato sayings in Italian, he wasn't sure she understood, but that he felt deeply. How good she felt. How much he loved being inside her. How he dreamed of her for almost a year. That she was his and he'd kill anyone who hurt her. That he loved her. He stopped himself then, thinking that maybe he was getting carried away.

Her eyes were glassy and unfocused, her breathing was ragged, ending on whispered sobs. Her body trembled and undulated, searching for release. With eyes locked and mouths locked, and bodies in perfect accord, Toni kept up his driving rhythm. Dani's hands traveled from his shoulders and torso to the base of his spine, and he felt her nails dig into his sides. She was close. He lifted her lower body again to meet his long strokes, sending her closer to the edge.

In a rush of breath, she shook under him and he felt her body clench around his shaft. He gave up control and lost himself in her body. They kissed all the way through it, both bowled over by the power of their sex and by the fierce symmetry of their orgasms. He gave and she took. She gave, and he was lost.

Toni emerged from his blinding climax knowing two things: she was still the best sex of his life. And he was never going to be able to keep his hands off her like he had promised.

The clock read 7 a.m., but sleep was elusive. After silently leaving Toni's bed, Dani found her scattered clothes and tiptoed upstairs to the kitchen. She made herself an espresso, wondering why she felt the need to pack her bags and run.

Because this was how it had started with Andre. And Martin. And her boyfriend from culinary school. And they all ended with someone getting hurt, namely her.

She pulled in a deep breath and told herself this time

was different. Her time with Toni was limited and there was no time for feelings. They had four more days to get ready and a laundry list of things to prepare.

They'd had a lapse in judgment. But it didn't have to affect their working relationship. *Just stay focused*, she told herself, *and don't let your feelings get out of control*.

Feelings? She slumped against the counter and sipped her Italian roast, staring out the window over the green hills and into the purple horizon. *Do I have feelings for him?* she asked the sliver of sun peeking from behind the mountains.

Her gaze landed on the lush garden and meticulous rows of wine grapes. She couldn't run, but maybe a walk would do her good. She zipped up her hoodie and slipped her feet into a pair of wellies in the mudroom, then with coffee in hand stomped past the greenhouse and through the garden into the vineyard.

She couldn't help but finger the dew-covered leaves and grapes as she slowly strolled through the labyrinth. Wine had always been a complement to her dishes, but seeing the little grape that would eventually become the beverage of the gods was awe inspiring.

"Hey, little grape. You're going to make someone very happy one day."

She fingered the dew, the droplet somehow reminding her of Toni and how wonderful he was with his fingers. And his body. And his lips. He'd whispered Italian in her ear, making her go a little crazy for him. She didn't recognize all of it, too engrossed in how good he felt, but she thought she'd heard *Sono innamorato di te*. "I'm in love with you."

An inner voice told her to stop being ridiculous. If he did say that, it was in the moment. Andre would tell her that during sex all the time. It meant nothing, clearly. And Toni didn't love her. She was only there for a little while. They were just acting on impulse, and now that it was out of their systems, they could begin working together like adults. Adults who didn't have any more sex.

"Angel, it's freezing. What are you doing?"

She jerked, splashing lukewarm coffee on her hand. Toni approached in wellies and his pajamas. His bed hair stuck out at all angles, making him look sexier than anyone should so early in the morning. The events of their night rushed back to her. The feel of him, the weight of him, the length of him inside her. Heat rushed across her skin.

She bit her lip. Just one look at him. That's all it took. Her heart sped up as he got closer, then it jumped when he smiled. No, she couldn't have this reaction. Not if they were going to work together.

And not if she was going to leave Italy unscathed.

"Hey" was all she could muster. He reached for her, but she pretended to be checking herself for more spilled coffee and moved away, trying to get away from him and the electrically charged space that now swirled around them. Suddenly she wanted to touch him. And him to touch her. Just one kiss, she mused keeping her distance from him before mentally slapping herself.

From the corner of her eye, she saw him stop and put his hands on his hips.

"I don't like waking up alone."

"I was craving coffee."

He stared at her. "Trying to avoid me?"

His deep voice was thickened by sleep and sex.

"Of course not. I just needed a walk." She sipped her coffee, which had gone almost cold, and tried to find her voice.

"You're having regrets."

"No." It was true. She didn't regret it. But she was afraid he would.

"Then come back to bed." His voice was patient and his fingers grazed her elbow as if testing the waters. Then she was there in his arms and his lips were on hers. She held her coffee cup out to the side while he ate at her mouth and wrapped his arms around her waist. He didn't let go of her mouth as his palms smoothed over her bottom.

Had they been in his room, she might have given in, instead she gathered all the inner strength and wiggled from his arms.

She turned her back to him and caught her breath. Then she turned. His dark brows were scrunched and his chest rose and fell rapidly.

"What was that?"

"Your daughter and mother are around."

"They're in bed, where we should be."

"Toni, last night was great, but I think we should acknowledge last night for what it was."

"You mean this morning." His brows went up. "And what was it?"

"The last time. We have other priorities to focus on and sex would get in the way. We're expected to work together, not sleep together."

She was handing him an out on a silver platter. Later he would realize that he wasn't that interested in her. That she wasn't his type.

"We can do both."

"I can't."

"Try."

She chuckled at his insistence. "I don't want your mother to get the wrong impression."

"And what impression is that? That we like each other? That we made love several different ways hours ago? That would be the right impression."

"I don't want her to think that we are together or dating or whatever Italians do."

"They get married."

"Well, we're definitely not doing that."

His gaze didn't waver, and then he smiled a slow smile and held out his hand. "Come back inside."

"I won't be your lover and your chef, Andre." Dani's hand went to her mouth.

"Andre? I am not Andre." Toni closed the distance between them and cupped her cheek. "I'm *not* Andre."

"I know. I don't know why that came out like that."

"What are you afraid of?"

"Of being a cliché."

Toni cocked his head at the strange answer.

"How can I help you not become a cliché?"

"By pretending that last night didn't happen."

Toni's lips became a thin line.

"Fine. We can act like nothing happened." He pulled her face toward his and gave her a searing kiss. Then he looked into her eyes. "But we both know it did."

He dropped his hands and walked back to the house, leaving her feeling bereft and unsteady.

Chapter 15

Grace and Sophia watched under frowns of confusion while Dani and Toni barely spoke to each other over breakfast. The silence got even louder when they walked out the door toward Via Olivia.

Dani's skin prickled with magnified awareness as Toni followed her down the cobblestone path from the villa to the restaurant. The path crested and before her she saw the sprawling one-story building made of glass and stone that sat majestically behind another garden of wildflowers, small ponds and a white statue of three dancing ladies.

"They are the Graces," Toni said, following her eye line.

"They look…graceful."

"You'll see more when we visit the museum."

Her stomach flip-flopped at the term *we*. He strode past her toward a large wooden door, but Dani stopped and let her gaze roam the property. She could see why this was ten years in the making. Gravel paths with benches were folded into the greenery and she could see the surrounding trees in the distance that shielded the estate from sight.

The veiled gem rivaled a king's country home. Dani traveled up the small steps to the main entrance where Toni stood. He was in jeans and a light sweater, and a light fragrance of pine lingered around him.

She'd smelled the same subtle fragrance on his skin when they had slept together and she fought the memories that flooded her thoughts.

"How are people going to find this place?"

"A map. There is a parking pavilion through those trees." His outstretched arm revealed a beautiful stone archway at the side of the building. "It's secluded, that's part of the appeal. And you should see it at night. There are lights in the walkways and hidden in the garden." He sent her a look. "It's romantic."

She bet. Her gaze landed on a glass room where wine bottles were artfully stacked.

"Is that a tasting room?"

"*Sì*. Come, Chef. You can taste anything you like." She ignored the comment, but she felt it in her panties. He held open the door and she slipped by him, feeling overly conscious of his presence.

"Nice bar," she said. The cherrywood gleamed. Toni smiled with pride and slapped a hand on the top.

"It's sturdy too." He looked at her under lowered lids. Suddenly her clothes felt too small.

"Good, then it can support a lot of drunk rich men."

"It can support more than that."

She looked him up and down.

"Are you trying to have sex with me on this bar?"

"*Sì*, Chef. I would love to have you spread out on this bar."

Dani fought her rising arousal. "That sounds unsanitary."

"But worth the health inspection, I bet."

"Toni. This is not what we discussed."

He straightened. "*Sì*, Chef."

"Show me…the kitchen."

His grin was mischievous. "*Sì*, Chef."

He acted as tour guide as they made their way through the complex.

"There are four dining rooms that face the back garden. All are connected." She stopped to study the elegant interior ripe with gilded wallpaper, perfectly set tables and crystal chandeliers. "A guest lounge." They passed a room with a fireplace and leather seating. "Guest washrooms are there and cell phone stations are there. We have separate areas for the staff."

Dani was impressed. Accommodations for staff were usually subpar.

"Who keeps this place together? It's immaculate." Someone had to be overseeing the space.

"Mamma, Marcello and I take turns. But if you're talking about staff, they are local people. We pay them well to be invisible, but only to the guests."

Toni made a turn toward the back of the room then out into a beautiful secluded patio where Dani counted fifteen staff members standing in a row, silent and still.

"Staff, I'd like you to meet Danica, our chef. Marcello would have no other here so please treat her with the respect that you would him."

They bowed in unison and one stepped forward. "*Benvenuto*, Chef."

"*Grazie*. It is an honor. You've outdone yourselves."

Toni went down the line and impressively introduced each of the members by name and background. When he was done and the staff dismissed themselves, Dani turned to Toni with a smile.

"You know them all."

"We are a sustainable restaurant. That means the people need to thrive here too."

Never had she felt so attracted to a man than at that moment.

His gaze lingered on her lips, and then he swallowed and continued. "This is the outside staff lounge. There is a den below these stairs with an inside lounge."

Dani followed Toni down the stairs and peeked her head through a wood door. Leather couches and a Persian rug graced the inviting space. Rows of unisex restrooms lined one wall and a cell phone station sat in the corner. Along with a laptop station.

"I can see myself taking a long break in here."

"I can see you naked on that couch."

Dani hitched her hands on her hips. "Is that all you think about? Sex?"

His brow went up. "When you're this close and no one is around? *Sì.*"

He leaned closer and she moved backward until her back was against the wall. He placed one hand on the wall by her head and half caged her with his body.

"You look delicious."

She made a dismissive noise. Knowing she wanted to test the kitchen, she'd thrown on a V-neck T-shirt and had put her hair in a ponytail. "I look like a farmhand."

His eyes dipped into the V of her shirt, making her breathing increase slightly. He hadn't even touched her, yet her body was screaming for him. His knowing gaze came up to hers.

"What would you do if I kissed you right now?"

"I'd leave."

He frowned. "Really? I don't think so."

"I thought we were going to cultivate our working relationship."

"We are." His lips moved closer and their breaths mingled.

"I thought we were going to forget what happened."

His fingertip ran down her arm. "Can you forget, angel? Because I'm having a hard time."

She shivered, not sure when the name went from an annoyance to an endearment she craved hearing.

They heard steps on the patio and Toni stepped back just in time for the doors to swing open. Two of the staff members she just met headed toward the restroom. Toni held her gaze as he opened the door.

"Come. Your kitchen awaits."

Just off the dining rooms and the rear gardens was a tall vented stand-alone building. They walked the wide path from the main building into swinging doors and Dani gasped at the silver and white beauty before her.

Marble countertops, prep islands, chopping stations, stainless steel appliances and heat lamps, copper cookware, ceiling fans, and hanging from shiny hooks were rows of white coats, with two black ones at the end.

She was home.

Her gaze scrolled over the burners, imagining bubbling sauces and sizzling meats and— She turned when she heard the door open.

"Where are you going?" Toni had one foot out the door.

"Letting you get acquainted. Your staff will be here in an hour. I'll be in the tasting room. Text if you need me."

He winked and left, leaving her a little speechless. How did he know she wanted to be alone with the kitchen? The memories of him driving himself inside her came from nowhere and she ran a hand over the cool marble as a distraction.

She thought she could forget, but her body was having none of that. She wanted him. Again. Would that set her free? One more time? Ten more times? She gritted her teeth and let her fingertips guide her to the ovens.

She spied a small alcove and delighted in all of the full freezers and jar storage. She smelled the dried herbs, inhaling long and hard to wipe away any thoughts of Toni.

She only had days to whip her kitchen into shape. She needed a way to get him out of her system.

An hour later the kitchen staff trickled in. Dani introduced herself to the handpicked selection of cooks who had worked with Marcello in the past and present. She recognized one or two from Via Carciofo, then outstretched her hand to Dao, a small Japanese man with a stern face. Marcello's other sous-chef, now hers.

"Chef." He bowed. Dani frowned at the thought of a Japanese chef in an Italian restaurant, but then, some had said she never belonged in an Italian restaurant, either. It made you work harder. She had a feeling they would get along well.

After introductions she put them to work, giving them a task of preparing five simple Milanese dishes of their choice. A test, so to speak. She watched silently and they worked efficiently, taking Dani's instruction where she saw fit to give it. Save one.

The French saucier looked at her tattoos and sneered.

"I came here to learn from a top chef, not a prep cook who slept with Andre Pierre."

Rage boiled under Dani's skin, but before she could act, Dao grabbed a French rolling pin, yelled in Japanese and cracked the long wood on the counter.

"Apologize!"

The room gaped and the saucier's eyes went wide. The Frenchman's gaze shifted back to Dani, and then he whispered, *"Désolé."*

Dao stepped forward. "Out!"

The saucier looked to the room for support, but none extended even a look. His spoons clattered as he shoved his pots away and tossed his coat on the floor.

The room stayed silent as he took his bag from the lockers by the door and swung wide the double doors.

"Chef, on behalf of the staff, our sincere apologies." Dao bowed again.

Dani made no movement, but inside she shook. The way he looked around for support meant things had been said. This staff thought she was a joke.

Dani grabbed the saucier's discarded pot and threw it

across the room. Tomato basil puree splattered the white brick as if remnants from a murder.

"Who else would like to leave?" Her raised voice echoed. "Go." She tossed another pot. "Go!"

No one moved. Her laser gaze hit everyone in the room.

"I don't care what you've heard or what you've read. You are here because you were handpicked by Marcello. And so was I! When you let me down, you let Marcello down. Now get back to work!"

All turned their backs quickly and focused on their stations. Head high, Dani slowly walked out the doors, took a deep breath, and then she felt the pull of tears rising from her throat.

She clutched her forearm and dug her nails into her skin, hoping to distract herself with pain. But her scarred and tatted arm was bulletproof, and she chuckled at her feeble attempt.

The tear subsided and as her fingers slid over the bumps in her arm she remembered that she'd paid her chef's dues over and over. They didn't just give out Michelin stars at Walmart. Unfortunately, her name wasn't attached to any of them.

It's her fault. Not Andre's, hers. She let him take the credit. She let herself be a ghost.

She didn't want to be a ghost anymore.

"We're ready, Chef." Dao's voice was low behind her.

"I'll be right in." She tossed over her shoulder. "And good work." She wanted to hug the man, but as second in command it was his job to keep the staff under control. If he hadn't have stepped in, *she* would have had to fire *him*.

Dani heard the door swing shut and she waited only a minute more on purpose, just to remind everyone that she could. Moving to go back in, her gaze swept the windowed dining area in appreciation, but she stopped midturn when she recognized Ava's blond hair and slender form in the guests lounge.

She was standing in a formfitting dress, looking every bit the hot girl, staring out over the garden when Toni walked into the room and handed her a glass of wine. They sat together on one of the leather couches and Dani tried not to let the fingers of jealousy tighten around her throat.

They could be talking about Sophia or taxes or…enemas. Whatever they were saying, they looked cozy. Dani felt a prickle of insecurity. Women loved Toni, just like Andre. *Hot girl, Hot guy.*

When Dani walked back into the kitchen, five dishes were lined up under the heat lamps, and the staff was standing against the wall. Dao handed her a fork and stood behind the first dish for Dani's inspection. They were seasoned cooks, but learning a new menu still took practice. She bent over each dish and graded for presentation, preparation, creativity and taste.

"The orecchiette is rolled perfectly." She popped one in her mouth. "Too much lemon juice in the pasta water. The broccolini is bit overdone and I'd want a bit more of a crust on the sausage. Could have been browned half a minute more." With each tip, Dao nodded his head. She speared a burst tomato. "Nice tomato. Overall, not bad."

She moved onto the next dish, a risotto in lemon and olive oil. She tasted it and then tossed the dish. "Overcooked." The third and fourth dishes received the same fate, but the fifth dish, a Swiss chard ravioli was almost perfect.

She stood and looked at Dao. "We have a lot of work to do. I want everyone here tomorrow afternoon."

Dao bowed.

It was 1 a.m. when Dani found her way to the restaurant kitchen, unable to get that saucier's sneer, nor the vision of Toni and Ava drinking wine together, out of her mind. She wasn't jealous, she told herself when she flipped on the burners and splashed some oil into the pan. Chopped garlic sizzled while Dani lay sweet peppers one by one into the pan, watching for them to blister just right. She just didn't want to be played like a fool, like she was with Andre.

The smell of the simple dish calmed her nerves and her thoughts wandered to the launch and dishes she and her team had yet to perfect, to the servers she had yet to meet, to the wines she had yet to taste…which led her right back to Toni. She turned the shining peppers as flashes of their night together broke through her thoughts.

The slide of his hands on her skin, the trail of his lips over her breasts, the fullness of him inside her. He was relentless in his exploration of her body and she burned for it again.

Her mouth went dry. She flipped off the burners and shaved parmesan over the steaming dish. It melted beautifully like a snow-topped mountain. With her fingers she brought a pepper to her mouth and let her shoulders fall at the comfort. She reached for another pepper and stopped, thinking a light wine would complement her dish.

She walked through the darkened halls to the tasting room, hoping to find the wine locker open or maybe a few random wine bottles under the bar. She crossed the threshold and was surprised to find a few of the overhead lights illuminating just the bar area and four empty wineglasses on top.

"Hello?" Dani scanned the room and crept slowly toward the bar, wondering how the staff could have missed them. Could they have been Ava and Toni's glasses from earlier? *Looks like they had fun. Jealous much*, Dani chided herself. It was probably just— Dani jumped and let out a tiny yell when Toni appeared from around the corner.

"Toni?" Her heart hammered in her chest. "Oh my God, I thought you were a serial killer. What are you doing?"

"You mean lady-killer," he said with a smirk. "And I could ask you the same thing. But I won't." Dani lifted her brows at his flippant tone. His hair was messy and his pajamas were a little wrinkled, like he couldn't sleep. He eyed her for a second, letting his gaze travel unapologetically down her body. She was fully clothed in loose pajamas, but now she felt a little naked.

"Are you drunk?"

"Not yet." Toni popped a black bottle of wine and poured fizzing red liquid into the glass. His lips were a thin line.

"Are you okay?" She wondered if his behavior had anything to do with Ava.

"I will be when I drink this bottle. It's the Lambrusco made from our grapes. It arrived today."

"You're going to drink the whole bottle by yourself?"

He raised his glass to his lips and closed his eyes at the first sip. Nodding slowly as he savored the taste. His eyes popped open.

"No, you're going to join me. Taste." He pulled another glass from behind the bar and poured some for her. The fizz vibrated on her tongue. When she looked up he was watching her mouth.

"I'm up for one glass, but—"

"And then I'm going to make love to you."

"Wait...what?"

For all of her talk, you would think she would move when he stalked toward her. No, her body knew what it wanted and instead of weak protests, she threw her arms around his neck and kissed him like she was starving. She couldn't stop kissing him, couldn't stop feeling him. Their clothes came off in a frenzy, and then he lifted her and sat her on the counter. She wound her legs around him and he entered her in one hard thrust. She matched him kiss for kiss, thrust for thrust, their bodies moving in tandem, the erotic rhythm building until the first contractions of her body rippled against him. "*Ho un debole per te.* 'I'm weak for you.'" Toni's whispered words washed over her. They came together in a hot rush of entwined limbs and breathless moans.

Chapter 16

The next morning Toni and Dani drove to Milan to drop Sophia off at school and visit the markets to schedule deliveries for the opening at the end of the week. Dani scheduled lunch with her mother, but before then Toni made good on his promise to show her the Botticelli exhibit at the Pinacoteca di Brera gallery.

Venus stood comfortable and seductive in her half shell making Dani wonder if someone posed for the painting or if she was a figment of Botticelli's imagination. The collection, on loan from the Uffizi Gallery in Florence, was curated to focus on the artist's more pagan ideologies as the walls were filled with paintings of Greek and Roman mythology. Gods were square and muscular while the goddesses were fleshy and curvaceous. *Sensual*. Toni had used the term to describe Venus.

Dani had never felt that sensual standing nude in front of a mirror but there had been exceptions, recently. The things Toni had whispered in her ear the night before had made her feel sensual, and she had definitely been naked.

"His muse was the love of his life. But she was married to another," Toni murmured behind her. His breath at her ear left tingles down her spine, as did the way he laced his fingers into hers.

It wasn't supposed to feel this way.

She wasn't supposed to yearn for his touch or get excited when he brushed her arm. They had rules, which they had broken more than once, but just as the dawn broke through the clouds that morning they had agreed to focus. The launch was in four days and they didn't feel ready.

They may have sealed that pact with a kiss or two, but the minute she crept half-naked back to her room and closed the door, Cinderella had turned back into the maid, er, the chef.

"Venus was a real woman?"

"Her name was Simonetta Vespucci and she was a figure in several of his other paintings, as well. She died at age twenty-two. And he asked to be buried at her feet when he died."

"Isn't that a little rude? She was another man's wife."

Amused, Toni's gaze ran over her face. "Some would say it's romantic."

"Some would say crazy."

"There is no sense in love."

Toni led her by the hand and held it as they stopped in front of another painting.

Dani recognized Venus-Simonetta instantly in her pagan gowns. Then her gaze settled on the three scantily dressed women dancing to Venus's right.

"The dancers look like the statue at the restaurant. What did you call them? Graces?"

"Very good. It was a way for an artist to show the female body three ways simultaneously. There are statues like this throughout Rome. Full hips, round bellies." He pulled her closer to him and looked into her eyes. "Beautiful."

Dani licked her lips and tried to get her lust under control.

"How do you know so much about this?"

"I studied art history."

"Oh, I thought you would have studied business."

"I learned business from my family. But wine, the arts, music. I studied in college, and life."

"Music? Do you play an instrument?"

"I play a guitar."

"Of course you do."

"What does that mean?"

"It means I can see young Toni luring women with his smile and acoustic melodies."

"Well, I didn't have a bow like Cupid. I improvised."

Dani felt the atmosphere thicken. She knew all too well how good he was at improvisation.

Dani turned to the painting. Cupid hovered above Venus, but his bow was raised toward the Graces and a nearby unsuspecting male god reaching for an orange in a tree above him.

"Looks like someone is about to get lucky."

"I think you're about to get lucky."

Dani turned just in time to catch Toni's lips, and then he pulled back and looked into her eyes.

"Oops. Did I break the rules?" he said with a wicked smile.

"Yes." Dani looked around and saw only a few morning patrons. "We said we'd behave."

"Why does the word *behave* make people *not* want to behave?"

"I think that's just you."

"*Va benne*, angel." He kissed her hand, then let it go by her side. It felt cold suddenly. "Have I told you how beautiful you look this morning?"

Dani cocked a brow. He did tell her right before they had gotten into the car. He'd pulled her into his bathroom, locked them in and kissed her senseless. There were broken rules all over the place.

Dani chose an off-the-shoulder top for lunch with her mother. Toni trailed a finger over her exposed shoulder. "I like this top."

She shivered. Who was she kidding? Things weren't going to go back to the way they were. They had achieved a new level of intimacy and the only way to keep things neutral was to keep having sex. Dani swallowed hard.

"I think it's time for me to go."

"Don't run from me."

"I'm not running from you, I'm going to brunch with my mother. After ten minutes there, I guarantee I'll be running back to you."

"I like the sound of that." His smile faded. "Do you regret our sleeping together?"

"No, but I think we need to be careful. I don't want to upset Sophia or get your mother's hopes up."

"You're so logical. How did I not know this about you?"

"I think it's because your focus is usually just on yourself."

He feigned offense and gazed at her under narrowed lids. "Now you owe me one last kiss."

Her blood pulsed a little harder. "If I must."

Toni put his hand behind her head and pulled her mouth to his. She hadn't expected the raw sexual heat of his kiss or her own passionate response. They were in the middle of a semicrowded museum, and all she could think about was getting him naked and putting her mouth on his chest tattoo.

"Toni?"

Dani heard the small voice, then felt Toni stiffen and pull back. He twisted around and unblocked her view. There stood Ava, a snarl on her face, her eyes darting back and forth between her and Toni.

"It's not what you think," Toni said to Ava.

What? Dani flicked her gaze to the side of his face, studying his reaction as if she didn't hear what she thought she heard. Ava's gaze traveled over Dani, making her want to hide behind one of the statues.

"I know you…you're Francesca's daughter. The chef. You've really gotten desperate haven't you, Toni? First that teacher and now…"

"Ava!" Toni snapped. "Whom I spend time with is none of your business." Ava cocked her head and looked at Dani.

"He didn't tell you we were back together, did he?"

Toni stepped toward Ava, but she turned and hurried away, but not before giving Dani a disgusted look.

"Wait!" Toni called after his ex-wife, then whipped his head around to Dani as if suddenly remembering she was there. He didn't touch her, just stared at her as if he'd never seen her before. "I have to take care of this. Text me when you are done, we'll drive back."

He was gone just like that. As were the feelings she had been experiencing all morning. Suddenly her heart thudded like a rock and her skin felt grimy. Stupid top. Stupid girl.

She felt invisible. Maybe she really was a ghost.

Toni wasn't sure why he was running after Ava. Habit? Sophia? All he knew was that he didn't like the vindictive look in his ex-wife's eyes. The last time he'd seen her like this, he received a call from his lawyer saying Ava had filed for full custody. And by the way she snarled at Dani, Toni wasn't the only one on her shit list.

After he handled this, he'd find Dani and explain. The hurt and confusion that had passed over her face tore at his soul. What was Ava playing at? He needed this charade with Ava to end. He wanted stability. He wanted…Dani.

Toni caught up with Ava and cut her off before she hit the exit. A sadistic smile spread across her face at the sight of him.

He took her roughly by the elbow and led her to a less crowded corner. Then gritted his teeth as he spoke with barely leashed anger.

"What the hell are you doing here?"

"It's a public museum, Toni. And I love Botticelli too. Remember?" Toni stared at her, hard. "Fine, Grace told me you'd be here."

"What do you want?"

"I wanted to see you."

"No, you didn't. That jilted lover scene was beautiful, Ava. You should have pursued acting instead."

"Did you see the look on her face? Nobody wants a guy with a crazy ex. But really, Toni, I did you a favor. She's not your usual style."

"And they don't get crazier than you, Ava. And I thank God she's not usual. It's refreshing to date someone who isn't a complete narcissist."

Her eyes narrowed. "Be careful, Toni. Our custody arrangement can always change. But that's not what I want. I want you."

Toni rolled his eyes dramatically. He wanted to say that she must overestimate her mothering skills to think a court would choose her over him. He took the high road instead. "What is this, Ava? Are you in debt? Because I am having a really hard time believing that you still love me when you have been recently photographed with another man."

"Ha! You're jealous."

"Jealous? Is that why you did it? To get to me?" He grimaced. "Sophia saw that picture and cried. Doesn't our daughter factor into any of your schemes?"

Ava's smile deflated into a hard line. "You're the one with the live-in girlfriend at the moment. After you promised we'd work on our marriage."

"We are divorced! And I never agreed to work on us. I said I'd think about it. I decided the answer is no. Meanwhile, you were perfectly happy signing those papers when your lover was around."

He could see that by the shocked look on her face that his barb hit home, but instead of rail at him, she broke down. Her shoulders trembled as she bit back tears.

"I don't understand how we got here, Ava. One day you're happy to be a mother to our daughter, the next you were out at all hours of the night with strange men. Was a family life with me and Sophia so bad?"

Ava clutched at her chest and a quick rush of tears sat in her eyes. She dabbed at them with a manicured nail, checking to make sure no one saw. Her tears had melted his heart many times, but this time he wasn't going to let this go. The look of hurt and mistrust in Dani's eyes had infuriated him. Whatever was going on had to be squashed. Now.

"What do you want, Ava? What do you really want?"

She gave him a long look under thick, perfectly glued on eyelashes and darkened brows. She was camera ready at all times, and yet Toni didn't recognize her, not anymore. When did she go from a fresh-faced cover model to this heavily made-up ice queen?

"My life hasn't been the same since we divorced. You were always the stable one, picking me up when I fell down. I want that back, I want us back. It will be better for Sophia…"

"Stop acting like you want this for Sophia."

"I do think of Sophia! Every day!" Her hands shook as she pulled out a tissue from her purse and dabbed more at her eyes. "My contract is up soon and they are not going to renew. My publicist and I tried to stage a few stunts to get my name out there again, see if we could force them into keeping me, or attract another avenue. Reality TV maybe?" She giggled uncomfortably. "They wanted me to do a sex tape—"

"For the love of God, Ava."

"I said no, Toni. But I had to do something. So I went out to the most prominent parties, got photographed with men. I'm not sleeping with any of them, I just needed the PR."

He crossed his arms over his chest. "Did it work?"

"No. Your new girlfriend's mother is all anyone is talking about right now."

"She's an icon."

"She's old! It's ridiculous."

"This has nothing to do with me, so why are you pretending you want me back?"

"I'm not pretending. I'm going to retire. I'm going to change. We were good together once. You remember, I know you do." She slid herself into his arms, then stiffened when she saw something over his shoulder.

He followed her gaze and saw two suit-clad men in the doorway, their gazes where locked onto her. Slowly, she stepped away from him and righted herself.

"Who are they?"

"Um, drivers. I have a shoot today." She placed her tissue back in her purse.

"Think about what I said."

"About what, Ava?"

"About us."

Dani flashed in his mind. "No. There is no us. We are co-parents and…we could be friends, but no more."

"I don't believe that. You're just caught up in love again. It will be over soon. You'll come back to me."

"This is over, Ava." He said it with pointed distinction.

"It will never be over, Toni." She began to walk toward her drivers, then turned. "Oh, and good luck with the restaurant. I'll see you Friday night."

Toni's eyes widened. He'd forgotten that she received an invitation.

He checked the time and hurried back to the Botticelli exhibit. He'd promised Dani that he would drive her to brunch. If they hurried she could still make it. He rushed to where he last saw her. The crowd had thickened with tourists and art lovers, but there was no sign of her.

Chapter 17

Dani sat at the center table waiting for her mother and watched the ice melt in her water, reliving the way Toni ran after his ex-wife.

She hadn't been stupid enough to believe that the night before meant anything, so why was she so upset? A small gasp from the table beside her prompted her to look up.

Her mother wore large dark glasses and followed carefully behind the hostess in the tallest heels Dani had ever seen her in. The reverence on the hostess's face made Dani want to scream. She's a model for Christ's sake not the Pope.

"Nice shoes. I take it you won't be shopping today."

"That was yesterday. And you never know when you'll be photographed." Her mother's gaze shifted to the table behind Dani and she mouthed a gracious hello.

"Are we here to eat or boost your Instagram followers?"

Her mother's gaze locked with Dani's. "What's your problem?"

Dani was saved by their server, who read off the specials and nodded patiently while Francesca ordered something not on the menu, which only heightened Dani's annoyance.

"There is a menu, Mother, why don't you take a look at it?"

"Why should I when I know what I want? Chefs can cook anything, can't they?"

Francesca's tone rankled. The waiter diffused the tension by replying with an emphatic yes, taking Dani's order and quickly skirting the table.

Francesca cleared her throat and cocked her head. "You look very nice today. Is that lip gloss?"

"It's for your Instagram followers."

"What the hell has gotten into you?" she harshly whispered.

"Nothing. I just want Marcello to get better so I can go home."

"Back to your father?"

"No. Maybe I'll go somewhere else." Her mother narrowed her gaze.

"I've never seen you like this."

"Like what?"

"Sooo…indecisive. You've always known you wanted to cook. When you were a kid I'd come get you from the kitchen where Marcello was rolling pasta—" she chuffed "—but you would just cry when I showed up."

Dani managed a smile. "You told Marcello child slavery was illegal."

"Well, he wasn't paying you. And he said, 'she's not a slave, she's family.' Then he made you roll a few more tortellini."

Mother and daughter laughed, and then Francesca sobered. "You gonna tell me why you're in a mood?"

"I'm just tired."

"You slept with Toni, didn't you?"

"How the—" The food showed up; a small arugula salad with berries and two minuscule pieces of grilled chicken for her mother, and her risotto parmesan and Caprese salad.

Dani waited until all of the servers were out of earshot. "Why would you say that?"

"Your eyes are bloodshot like you didn't get any sleep and you're wearing a sexy top. I know all this skin isn't for me."

"So what if I did? It doesn't mean anything."

"Well, I'm happy to hear that, if it's true." Her mother's long look said she wasn't buying it. "Is it true?"

"Mmm-hmm."

"Oh Lord."

"What? I'm a grown woman."

"Who falls for every toxic man in a two-mile radius."

"Toxic? Is that why you warned him off?"

"Sharing secrets, huh? This is worse than I thought. Don't you see the similarities between him and Andre? Attractive, fast-talking, running around like a prince while you do all the work. Behind every good man *is* a good woman, because she allowed him to stand in front of her. You're just going from one disaster to the next."

"I'm really not sure I can take relationship advice from you, Mother. Regardless, you are taking this too far. I don't work for Toni, I'm just helping temporarily."

"Yeah, and every man loves temporary 'help.'"

"I can't believe you just said that to me."

"Let me tell you something, missy, you better hope Ava doesn't find out about you two. Talk about a bunny boiler. I'm convinced they modeled Glenn Close's character on her."

Dani closed her eyes. "She saw us kissing this morning."

"Oh Lord. What happened? Did she say something to you?"

"She ran off."

"Let me guess, he ran after her."

Dani closed her eyes and nodded. Just like Andre.

"You better end this."

"I will." Dani sipped her coffee, wishing she didn't care. "Tell me about your shoot." Her mother's phone rang and Dani prepared to be ditched when she saw it was Jessica, her mother's agent. But Francesca swiftly silenced the phone and went back to talking. The phone rang again.

"Mom, why are you avoiding your agent?"

"She's being insistent and I don't want to talk to her right now."

Dani's phone buzzed with an unknown number.

"I don't know who this is." Dani held up the phone.

"Let me see. The nerve of her!"

"Who is it?"

"It's Jessica. Don't answer it."

"What? How does she have my number?"

"I think you're my emergency contact."

"Oh. Well, maybe this is an emergency."

"It's not. Ignore it."

"Okaaay." Dani silenced the phone. But it rang again. "Mother, this is stupid. I'm going to answer it and tell her you're asleep or something."

"Just let it be—"

"Hello?"

"Danica!" Jessica squealed. "It's been so long, how have you been? Look, I need to talk to your mother, do you know where she is? *Vogue* won't wait any longer they need an answer. So, what did you think when she told you, were you nervous? Don't be nervous, it will just be one or two shots of you together but your mother will be on the cover, can you believe it? It's brilliant. I mean they are just piggybacking off of the Chanel campaign of course but to do a mother-daughter takes it a step further, don't you think? It would be you two, Cindy and her daughter, Claudia…"

The woman didn't take a breath and as Dani tried to piece together Jessica's rant, her mother began to look increasingly uncomfortable.

Dani frowned and briefly pulled the phone from her ear.

"Jess wants to know if we are doing the *Vogue* campaign."

"She's got nerve. Tell her no, we are not."

"She said you could get a cover."

"No."

Dani put the phone back to her ear and heard Jess still talking. "Hello? Danica?"

"I'm here. Umm, I'm not really sure—"

"No more unsure. Time is up, they need an answer today. You and your mother hash this out and call me back ASAP. I mean to be over fifty on the cover of *Vogue*. Huh! Are you kidding! Game changer! Okay, you two talk and call me back!"

Jessica hung up and Dani put the phone down.

"Sooo, Jessica wants to know if we are doing the *Vogue* shoot. She needs an answer today."

"She already has an answer. I told her no."

Her mother never turned down an editorial. Never. "Okaaay, but she mentioned a cover."

Francesca stopped chewing for a heartbeat, then stabbed another arugula leaf and shoved it in her mouth.

"It would extend my stay here by another week. I'm about ready to go home."

"Are you even going to tell me what it is? Maybe I'd like to do it?"

"You wouldn't like it."

"Try me."

Her mother shrugged. "It's a mother-daughter editorial. Just a few full page shots with a small interview attached."

"And the cover…"

"I suppose, but that's never a given. Beyoncé could break a heel on stage tomorrow and the whole thing could be replaced by an in-depth interview about how her wardrobe malfunction made her feel."

A film reel of all the times her mother shooed her away from her work played in her mind.

"Still hiding me, huh, Mother?"

"And what does that mean?"

"It means you still can't deal with having a fat daughter."

"Danica, You are not fat. You're—"

"Full figured. So, you've said. I'm surprised you haven't tried to take this plate away from me."

"Well, there is too much cheese, if you ask me."

Dani's shoulders slumped. "And of course you have jokes. Because a supermodel having a fat daughter is funny."

"My decision not to do the shoot has nothing to do with you! You're just upset because you got loved and left this morning. Don't take that out on me."

The sting of her barb turned into a burn. "Okay, then let's do the shoot."

Francesca blinked. "Don't you have to open that restaurant?"

"I'm sure I can make room."

"No. You just want to do the shoot because I don't want to. This is my career and I won't take jobs on a whim."

Dani jumped from her seat. "I can't win with you, can I. Or at anything else for that matter. Goodbye, Mother."

"Sit down. You're embarrassing me."

"Well, what's new? I've always embarrassed you, haven't I?"

Fuming, Dani left her mother in the restaurant and hailed a taxi. She'd been a fool, not once, not twice, but three times. First Andre, then Toni, and now her own mother. Dani stared out the window as they sped toward the hotel. To be fair, her mother hadn't changed; Dani just wasn't in the mood to placate her anymore. Or anyone, for that matter. She really *was* attracted to toxic, wasn't she? But then each one of these issues had a common denominator…her. She had to stop allowing toxic into her life.

Her phone vibrated with Toni's calls and texts, which she ignored, even the ones that said he was sorry. He'll be sorry when she doesn't come back to the restaurant, she thought. But in her heart she knew she would never go that route. One thing she wasn't was a quitter and she really did feel that restaurant could be great. She just had to get through a few more days with Toni, but for that she'd need some help.

Ignoring several more texts, Dani picked up a few personal items from the hotel then took a car to the hospital. Marcello's weak smile tugged at her heart. He looked gaunt and tired, the planes of his jovial face shadowed and sunken. The strength of his grip when she held his hand had waned and Dani did her best to keep her concern from her face. He didn't look good and she was afraid he would never make it out of that bed.

"Bella, you look worried. You must tell me everything." And aside from her concerns for his health, she did. She told him about the restaurant, how she felt about Toni and the issues with her mother. It felt like old times and as always, Marcello gave her guidance. "Dani, you are finished being a ghost, which you have been with both Andre and your mother. Step into your light and things will fall into place. That's all you have to do. Toni is waiting for you."

Dani blushed. "Toni has ex-wife drama."

"Toni thinks keeping Ava happy will keep his daughter happy." Marcello waved his hands in the air. "He wants everyone to be happy, but he never focuses on himself. But he is beginning to see himself with you, I saw it when you were here together."

Could she have misinterpreted Toni's need to run after his ex? Marcello broke into her thoughts.

"Your mother came to see me a few days ago. She thanked me, if you can believe it. She is proud of you, Dani."

Dani's head snapped up. "That woman is full of pride, but not for me."

"She said it herself," her mentor said with a gentle gaze. "She knows she wasn't the most nurturing parent, but you get your drive and determination from her, Dani. She is the reason why you are a survivor."

Marcello handed Dani a tissue as the tears began to fall. She squeezed her eyes shut and wiped her nose, and when she opened them, there stood Toni, his gaze full of remorse.

"It wasn't what it looked like," Toni said, stepping farther into the room.

"That's what you said to *her*." Dani hated the way her voice shook.

"I just don't want her to hurt you."

"I can handle her."

Toni gave her a lopsided smile. "I know. I'm sorry."

Dani stood and stepped into his arms. He hugged her tight, placing kisses in her hair, murmuring how stupid he was. He kissed her, sweetly at first, then more deeply, until a deliberate sound of someone clearing their throat interrupted. Dani pulled away and caught Toni shamelessly winking at his uncle. Dani's gaze followed Toni as he greeted his uncle with kisses. She caught herself smiling, then lost that smile as her phone vibrated with a text from her mother.

We are doing the photo shoot. Jessica will give us the details. I hope you are happy now.

I am. Thank you. I love you.

I love you too.

Marcello was right, it was time to step into her light.

Chapter 18

Days later, Dani was standing in the restaurant kitchen, impressed. Marcello's pasta chef, a sixty-year-old woman with poor hearing, rolled a perfect sheet of dough and began slicing off precise strips of linguini by hand. *Perfetto.* Slowly Dani strolled past the staff, touching and tasting, praising and correcting.

They had been at it all week, perfecting a rhythm, getting to know the kitchen and each other. Now they had twenty-four hours until the soft launch and all were aware that Marcello was counting on them. Day and night they were in the kitchen working on versions of the dishes they plucked from Marcello's menu book. It kept her busy, too busy to think about Toni.

After the incident at the museum, they had come to a new understanding. They were dating for however long she was staying in Milan. No more rules or denying feelings. It would have been idyllic, except Toni had an emergency at one of his warehouses and stayed in Milan for a couple days.

There had been some sexting and a few filthy phone calls, but it wasn't enough to quench her need to touch him in the flesh. He'd arrived hours ago, hell-bent on making love to her, until he saw the dining room staff waiting for him.

Dani lifted her head to stare into the dining room. Toni was introducing the wines to the waitstaff. She couldn't hear him and watched as he poured tastings into each of their glasses and spoke animatedly with his hands.

She had to admit, the reprieve allowed her some much-needed kitchen time, and it showed. The staff was coming together nicely. Now all they needed to do was step into *their* light.

Standing off to the side, Liam caught her looking and gave her a cheeky wink. She returned his teasing with a frown and quickly turned, running headlong into her sous-chef carrying a rack full of lemon tarts. Her white coat looked like a Jackson Pollock painting.

"I'm sorry, Chef."

"No, Dao, it's my fault." She swiped some of the tart from her jacket. "That's pretty good."

"Is everything all right?"

Her heart thudded uncontrollably at Toni's voice. She only half turned.

"We're fine. Just a dessert mishap."

Toni moved closer, stuck his fingertip in one of the broken tarts and sucked the filling from his finger.

"That's divine." He picked up the tart. "May I?"

"Of course."

He took a bite. Dani tore her gaze from his lips and took the opportunity to skirt away. But he was right behind her, licking his fingers.

"Can I talk to you?"

He was wiping his hands on a towel when she turned and looked at him. He was casual in an old soccer jersey that hugged his biceps. His clear gaze was questioning.

She nodded and bit her cheek against her body's memory of how good he felt against her.

"Step into my office," he joked. He followed her into the meat locker, the only place in the kitchen with privacy.

"What's up?"

"How is Dao doing?"

"Great. He's very efficient. I see why Marcello chose him."

"Good."

There was a long pause before Toni moved toward her. "You're really close."

"It's cold. I'm conserving heat."

She stepped back and found herself against a leg of lamb. "Is there more to discuss?"

"My mother is coming back tonight. She is picking up Sophia and they are going to join us for dinner."

"A trial run? Okay, that's great."

"Is the kitchen ready?"

"Should I be insulted that you just asked me that?"

"You did just have an accident."

"We're getting used to the space. We're ready. I just wish Marcello could have blessed the menu."

"The menu looks perfect." Toni's chilled breath brushed her ear as he leaned closer. "What would you do if I kissed you right now?"

She was finding it hard to breathe. "I'd run screaming."

"Would you?" He chuckled, leaning in. "Did you think about me while I was gone?"

"No," Dani whispered, fighting the urge to touch him.

"Liar. Sophia passed her last test."

"Good for her."

"I told her to bring that boy to the launch. I want to meet him."

"Oh right. Now she is free to enjoy the opposite sex again."

"I was thinking of letting you enjoy me."

"Oh, just being considered is enjoyment enough."

"Dani, you can't avoid me forever," he said, his voice as thick as honey.

"I'm not avoiding you, I'm working. As you should be," she teased.

She pushed him aside, letting her fingers linger a little too long on his chest as she moved past him.

"Let me know when they get here," she tossed over her shoulder before exiting the freezer.

A few hours later Dani was finishing the garnish on a chocolate cake when she saw something whizz by the window to the garden.

Stretching her neck, she saw a blur of long dark hair and long legs stop a soccer ball, then execute a massive volley. Dani moved closer as Sophia fished a ball from the bushes, then threw it back out.

Dani inhaled when Toni ran into her view, expertly maneuvering the ball and kicking it back to his daughter. Despite the chilled afternoon, Toni had removed his shirt, giving Dani a reminder of just how hard his torso was.

Her lips had been all over that tattoo.

Sophia spotted Dani watching. She jumped up and waved at the window, prompting Toni to wave, as well. Dani blushed at his slow smile and laughed when Sophia kicked a ball right into his chest.

Hours later Dani kept a watchful eye from the kitchen as Grace and Sophia were served their meal. Liam and Toni coached the staff from a distance while six courses were served and cleared. Grace sliced her fork into the last course, a chocolate cake garnished in a Lambrusco sauce she made from their family wine. Another bite was tasted, then sent away. Dani wrung her hands and made mental notes of all the things the kitchen could do better.

Timing, for one, the third course was late. Prepping, for another. The only parmesan left had been aged three years, she would have preferred the five-year. She heard footsteps in the hall outside the kitchen. Dani checked that the buttons on her coat were still buttoned, ready to defend herself. They'd only had days to prepare. The new saucier was excellent, but still learning the menu.

The staff froze when Grace burst through the double

doors, Toni, Liam and Sophia trailing behind. The stern look on her face said it all. Dani opened her mouth to apologize, but instead was wrapped in a strong bear hug then held her at arm's length.

"I prayed to the Virgin last night that Marcello would get stronger and that our restaurant would be a success. I heard nothing. Today, I saw her face in that velvet artichoke soup. And when I tasted it, I knew." Grace clapped her hands and smiled.

Dani waited for more, hoping that Grace's beaming face was a good thing.

"Mamma, please, just say you liked it." Toni winked at Dani.

"Liked it? I loved it! *Brava. Brava!*"

"I did too! I want more cake," Sophia piped up from her father's side, and Dao fixed her another slice.

Dani felt relief wash over her. "Grace, I know it wasn't perfect. But it will be. I promise."

"I'm going to get the champagne. We are celebrating!" Grace kissed both of Dani's cheeks and thanked the staff. Her praises to the heavens could be heard fading down the hall.

Dao snapped his fingers and the staff began to clean. Liam waved a goodbye while Toni walked to stand right in front of her. He leaned in a little and spoke for her ears only.

"If we were alone I'd kiss you right now."

"Is that all?" She was feeling good, flirty. Happy. And she began to recognize that look in his eye, just as her body began to automatically respond to it.

His gaze flicked to the long marble tabletop littered with flour and freshly rolled tortellini. "No, we'd have to break in this island."

"Like we did the tasting bar?"

"Exactly."

"I was thinking you could be spread out this time. That Lambrusco sauce might taste good licked from your torso."

He blinked and licked his lips, a glaze appearing over his eyes. Toni was a take-charge type of guy, which was evident in his life, and his sex. She'd wondered how he'd respond if she was the assertive one, and she reveled in his primal reaction, making her feel a bit like Venus in her half shell.

Dani caught movement out of her eye. Sophia was watching them. She took a deep breath and stepped back. "Sophia is done with her dessert. And she's watching."

"I'd like dessert." She knew he wasn't talking about chocolate cake.

"Dao, could you cut Toni a piece of cake. Extra Lambrusco sauce."

"You're lucky you're surrounded by people," he whispered. "If we were alone, I'd already be inside you."

Dani's insides went liquid.

Toni stepped back and took his plate. "Thank you, Dao. Nice job, everyone. My family and I can't thank you enough."

Grace returned with champagne and raised her glass to the staff. *"Salute,"* said the room and in that moment it felt like everything was falling into place.

The day of the soft launch was a blur and Toni was doing his best to keep everything together. The deliveries were late, a light rain started and several RSVPs still hadn't been confirmed. By the afternoon, the dining room tables were covered in white, soft music lilted through the air, and the lighting inside and outside of the restaurant was romantically staged. Fresh flowers perfumed the hallways, the bar was filled and the wine locker was open. Their well-trained staff manned each room. Toni caught a glimpse of himself in the hallway.

His navy suit was impeccable and hid the fact that he was sweating, hard. Quick steps led him to the kitchen doors. He peered through the window and found Dani in her black coat and Crocs, vigorously stirring a pot and yelling out orders. He smiled when he saw Sophia in a white coat in the corner with the pasta chef.

"Don't stare, you'll make her nervous," his mother said behind him.

"How is she doing?"

"Wonderfully. I've sneaked in and tasted a few things. Brilliant. Just brilliant. This is going to be a defining moment. I can feel it."

Toni wished he could mimic his mother's optimism. The critic from *The Taste* had not RSVP'd. Maybe it didn't matter. The man moved in secret, so there was a possibility he could show up. But that wasn't his only problem. His ex-wife was definitely coming. He just prayed she didn't make a scene.

Dani caught Toni at the window and lifted her brows, a silent question. He just smiled and shook his head, then blew her a kiss. She blew one back, then got back to work. He nodded his head, a defining moment indeed.

Dani wiped her brow and took a slow steady breath. Basil, oregano, paprika, she began her calming ritual just as they were putting the finishing touches on the third course. So far everything was going smoothly and from her vantage point, Dani could see that the dining rooms were full. A few beautiful people lounged in the tasting room and she caught a few journalists trying to get a peek into the kitchen, but Grace was like a gentle bear, directing everyone back to the main house. Dani turned back to her food, trying to ignore the fact that her mother still hadn't shown up.

"Dani, are you going to stay now?"

Sophia carefully placed each pasta roll into the boiling water while Dani concentrated on getting just the right spices in her white sauce. "What do you mean, love?"

"I mean, are you still going back to New York?"

"Well, I'm not sure about New York, but once this is up and running and Marcello comes back, I'll have to figure something out."

"You could stay here, in Milan."

"I doubt it, sweetie, Milan doesn't need any more chefs," she chuckled, focusing on the food, unaware of Sophia's frown and the slump of her shoulders. Dani heard the double doors of the kitchen open and expected to see Grace.

She froze when Andre slowly walked farther into her kitchen, a smile on his face that didn't reach his eyes.

"What the hell are you doing here?" Her staff faltered at his presence, but Dani gave them all a look to keep working.

"I was invited," he said, his voice as smooth as dirty silk.

"No, you were not. Get out."

"Actually, I'm here with the editor of *Good Food*, she got the invite. You look well. The food is…it's fantastic."

"If you have something to say, say it, then please leave."

"I'm sorry. Bette and I are no longer together. The TV show fell through. Actually, it's all falling apart. We lost a Michelin star since you've left. I came to ask if you would consider coming back. The staff needs you."

Dani's mind raced, unsure if what she was hearing was real. Andre there apologizing. It was what she dreamed of, and yet she didn't care. She wasn't even going to dignify his question with an answer.

"If that's all, please go. We are busy."

His head hung, and then he nodded. "Maybe we can

talk later," he murmured before slipping through the doors. Grateful he didn't cause a scene, Dani turned toward Sophia, but the young girl was gone.

Just as the fourth course was being served, Dani ran downstairs to the staff restrooms. The next course of entrées was running through her mind when she ran headlong into a tall blonde in a fur coat. Ava. What the hell was she doing down there?

"You," she sneered. "I can understand him wanting something a little different, but you're not even on the spectrum, are you?"

"If you are talking about the spectrum where a smart woman can feed a man when he's hungry and has enough curves to satisfy a man when he needs it, then you and I aren't even on the same planet."

Ava's eyes glittered with hatred. "I'm going to get him back."

"No, you won't."

Dani grinned at Ava's wide eyes, and then she left the model there to stew while she used the ladies' room. She had a job to do and Ava wasn't going to get to her anymore.

Dani rushed back to the kitchen only to find Dao in a frenzy.

"A woman came in looking for Sophia, then told the staff they were doing a horrible job. I led her out."

Dani let out an exasperated breath. Ava. She should tell Toni, but there was no time. "That was Sophia's mother. You did the right thing, Dao. I don't think she'll be coming back. Let's get the fifth course ready."

"Chef!" Liam stood just inside the doors holding four plates of entrées. His eyes wide with horror. "They are sending them back."

Dani's heart seized. "What? Why!"

The server tossed the plates on the island. "Too spicy."

Dani grabbed a fork and jammed the food into her mouth. She spit it out. Then tried the other three. All the same. Cayenne pepper. But how? The spice was burning her mouth, just like she could feel her career and the restaurant burning up in flames. She slumped over the entrées ready to cry. She looked up from the island to see Toni just inside the doors, his face like stone.

Chapter 19

Toni showed the last of their guests out of the door, found a single malt scotch under the bar and drank straight from the bottle. He took another swig as his gaze slid to the windows and locked on the lights of the kitchen. Ten years he'd been building this and it was already crumbling after one night.

He could see it now. The bad reviews would trickle in tomorrow, leaving a black mark on his family's reputation. He was avoiding the kitchen, unsure that he was ready to talk to Dani.

What the hell happened?

Everything had been going perfectly. The food editor of *The Evening Standard* had even pulled him aside and raved. But that was before the fourth course. He looked toward the window and saw bussers and servers taking plates back to the kitchen.

Few guests had stayed for the seventh course and those that did had left several dishes untouched. By the start of the dessert course, the dining room was near empty. Toni jerked off his tie and took another deep drink.

He wanted to scream at her and yet his body yearned to hold her. He knew she was just as distraught. This wouldn't bode well for her reputation either.

After another pull from the bottle, he looked up and caught a glimpse of Dani through the opened doors. Her hands were on her face and her fingers were wiping her eyes. Was she crying? His feet were in motion before he could think to stop himself. He was making quick work of the hallway when he spotted Sophia holding herself in the corner.

"*Cara mia*, you should be in bed."

"I want to go home, Papà."

"Nonna left the back door open. You can go—"

"No, I want to go home. I want to sleep in my own bed." Toni frowned. Her eyes were puffy as if she'd been crying and she wasn't meeting his eyes. He felt guilty suddenly that she was being affected by the family troubles.

He'd met her—dare he say it—boyfriend earlier in the evening and although he still had his misgivings, he seemed like a decent boy. Some chaperoned "dates" could be arranged, but that was it.

"Sophia, I don't want you worrying about this."

"But Mamma said the restaurant will fail now." Toni gritted his teeth at Ava's loose tongue.

Grace appeared and put her hands on her hips. "Nonsense. No one listens to those critics anymore. We will open next week as planned. I don't care what they write. It was a soft launch for a reason. Nothing is perfect on the first night."

Toni nodded his head at his mother's bolstering pep talk, but their exchanged glances over Sophia's head said otherwise. His gaze shifted over his mother's shoulder toward the kitchen.

"Mamma, what happened?" He asked low.

"My love, I don't know. I'm telling you, everything was perfect. She was fantastic. Go talk to her."

"I am, I just—" He shook his head. "I don't know what to say."

"Don't yell at her, Papà." Sophia wiped at her eyes and he again felt that she didn't need to be around the drama. Maybe it was best that he took her back to Milan.

"I'm not going to yell at her. Come, I'll take you home."

When Toni looked up, Ava was standing off to the side with a martini in her hand.

"I'll hitch a ride, too, if you don't mind." Toni didn't like that snide, satisfied look on her face. It gave him the feeling that she had something to do with the night's events. Grace gave Ava a once-over and left the hall.

"I thought you drove here," Toni said, wary of the little smile on her face.

"I took a car. I can't drive in these shoes." She did a little pose and pushed her stilettos forward. Then she held up her drink. "And I wanted to have a few of these."

He had wanted to speak to Dani first, but thought maybe a drive would cool his temper. They could talk when he got back.

"Fine. I'll get the car."

After a quick run to the main house, Toni parked in front of the restaurant. He left the car running as he got out and helped Ava down the stairs, her body swaying against his in what he felt were extra theatrics. After lowering her into the car, he made his way to the driver's side.

He had one foot in when the front door opened and Dani stood in her black coat and ponytail. The streaks on her cheeks almost pulled him from the car.

"You're leaving?" Her voice quivered.

"I'll be back."

They stared at each other for a moment, then he saw her gaze shift to the passenger side. He hated how it looked but had no choice. He told himself he'd explain later. He quickly ducked into the car, revved the engine and sped away.

The sun still hadn't risen when Dani woke in Grace's home. She groaned, that sunken feeling she'd had all night hadn't left her chest and her thoughts drifted to the sight of Toni driving away in the car.

He had been avoiding her. It was the only explanation for his not coming back to the kitchen. If only she could explain…what? That she had no clue how cayenne pepper made its way into her pasta sauce? It didn't matter how. She was responsible for the food. Ultimately it was her fault.

She had planned to wait for Toni at the restaurant, but after an hour she had decided to wait in her room. She figured he would find her there but he must have gone to his room. Dani tied her robe around her waist and went to look for him. She quietly opened the unlocked door and descended the stairs, her mind focused on what to say, but her explanation speech was forgotten when she saw that his bed was empty. And hadn't been slept in.

Ava. He was with Ava. She knew it in her bones. That image of him driving away in the car wasn't what bothered her, it was him driving away with his family. Ava was trying to get him back and what better way to do it?

Dani went back to her room and scrolled through her phone with hopes of a text from Toni. Nothing. There wasn't even one from her mother, who never showed. She swallowed back tears as she packed and zipped up her suitcase. Talk about getting kicked when you were down. If there was any other time when she felt like a ghost, this trumped them all.

Dani called a car service then left her bags at the foot of the stairs, intending to write Grace a note. There was so much to say. She had crumpled up three pages when Grace appeared in her robe. The older woman hugged Dani and tried to convince her not to leave.

"Please, stay. He'll come back and you can talk."

"He doesn't want to talk to me, Grace. I understand. The restaurant—"

"Bah! You think this is the first time our family has struggled? No. This will work out. But you and Toni, that's what I'm worried about."

Dani didn't know how to say it was just sex.

"We're not together, Grace."

Grace grabbed her shoulders.

"You're falling in love. Don't throw it away over this."

"No, we aren't. He's with Ava."

"He would never. I know my son."

Dani's phone chimed with a text that her car had arrived. Sure enough, a black car rolled slowly toward the house. Grace watched her with a pleading look in her eyes. Dani didn't want to disappoint Grace, but she needed to go. "Tell him I'm sorry."

Grace lowered her eyes then nodded. Dani grabbed her bags and shut herself away in the town car. During the ride she scanned the blogs for reviews, but none had posted yet. Doom was imminent, but for now she could ignore what was coming.

The closer the car got to her hotel, the more Dani thought about her mother's absence. And by the time she slipped her key card in the hotel room door, Dani was spoiling for a fight.

She found her mother in her infamous pink silk robe in front of the bathroom mirror peeling off a face mask. The surprise in her mother's eyes set Dani off.

"Too busy to come to your daughter's big night, huh?"

"Well good morning to you, too. What are you doing here so early?" Francesca asked Dani's reflection.

"That's what you have to say? You skipped my opening!" Francesca calmly put down her washcloth and turned around. Her mother's eyes held none of the concern she'd seen in Grace's eyes this morning, and it pissed her off. "Are you that ashamed of me?"

"Danica, I have never been ashamed of you."

The scathing laughter Dani let out came with a sneer. "Bull. You didn't come to the launch at Via L'Italy either? You've never once talked about me in your interviews. You prefer people not know that you have a daughter. I'm a black smirch on your perfectly manicured image. No one this fabulous could have a fat daughter who is a failing chef."

"Failing chef? What is this about? Did something happen last night?"

Dani blinked rapidly. "You're not listening to me."

Francesca stood from the vanity in the bathroom and walked past Dani to the breakfast table. She slid open a chair. "Sit down."

"No."

"Now!" Her mother's lips were a thin line.

Dani sat, biting her cheek, wondering why this woman still had so much power over her.

Her mother sat in a flurry of silk, angrily poured them both glasses of water, then took a deep breath and leaned in.

"Do you know what happens when I walk in a room full of press?"

"Mother—"

"Shut your mouth. Camera's pop out of nowhere, every one wants a quote, attention gets drawn away from the main event. My name gets splashed all over the press while yours gets buried. Your debut is important. I refuse to ruin that for my daughter."

Dani took a gulp of water, hoping she could drink the tears away. So many rebuttals and recollections of past hurts came to mind, but she shut her mouth and listened.

"I raised you to be a capable, independent woman. You don't need me there and I have a feeling you didn't even think about it until you were feeling unstable. You only look for me when something is wrong. So what's wrong?"

Oh God, she hated it when her mother was right. There was a moment when she had looked for her mother, but honestly her mother's presence was an afterthought. She felt like a bad daughter. Was this reverse psychology?

"No. No way, you are not going to do this to me. You didn't skip the opening for me. You were too busy. You are always too busy. Always working, where I am never allowed. Because you are ashamed that I'm not svelte and gorgeous like you."

Francesca frowned hard, her eyes filled with confusion. "Young lady, have you looked in the mirror lately?"

"Every day, Mother."

"And what do you see? Do you see what I see? What I know that Toni sees."

"Stop calling him *that* Toni—"

"You're beautiful, honey. Don't give me that look. You've always been beautiful."

"If you thought that you wouldn't have made me see your trainer."

"You were learning pastries that year and that's all you ate. It wasn't healthy!"

"See what I mean? You're always so critical of me. I know my weight is why you wouldn't let me come to your work."

Francesca sighed. "Not this again."

"So it's true."

"Danica, those people at my work are vultures. Yesterday I was told to only drink smoothies for a week. The samples don't fit me. I can't have my precious daughter with her grandmother's curvy figure anywhere near those fools. But I see it got to you anyway. It's my fault, I know. You see me starve myself and think I want you to look like this. But it couldn't be further from the truth. Never have I been ashamed of you."

"What about that time you told everyone I wasn't your kid?"

Francesca laughed. "You remember that? My agent told me to hide the fact that I had had a child. At the time the industry didn't want their cover girls being mothers. It promoted the wrong image, as if being a mother is wrong. But that's the way it was then. Christie had a baby and went from the cover of *Vogue* to the cover of *Ladies Home Journal*. Things are different now, hence our photo shoot together. Which is happening. So get ready. Once the cameras start they'll be telling you to suck it in, Photoshop this, stand this way so your wobbly bits look firm." The model rolled her eyes. "After all these years you'd think I'd be used to it. It's not what I want for you. That's why I didn't want to do the shoot."

Dani dabbed at her eyes. "Why have you never told me this?"

"You get defensive when I try to protect you."

Damn her mother's logic. "I love you, Mom."

"I love you too, baby. Now I'm going to order you some breakfast. Then you can tell me what's really bothering you."

Dani felt lighter as she ate and unloaded the event of the night. Her mother listened while sipping a fruit and kale smoothie.

"You were sabotaged. Sounds like Ava. I warned you."

Dani put down her fork. Could she have?

Her mother left the room to dress and Dani checked her phone. No calls or texts from Toni. Nothing. She was about to call him when her phone lit up with the Google alerts.

A Recipe for Disaster—The Daily Meal

Peppered with Brilliance—New York Magazine

Bittersweet to Taste—The Evening Standard

Dani read each review twice, her phone signaling more postings as she scrolled. The decor was praised while the food critiques were more specific about her failure. One thing was unanimous: they were delighted until the fourth course. Several of the articles skewed toward the idea that had Marcello been there, the disaster wouldn't have happened.

It was a silver lining for the restaurant. The critics had faith that once Marcello got back into the kitchen the restaurant would be spectacular. Dani chose one of the better reviews and texted it to Toni, disappointed when he didn't respond.

Danica Nilsson had failed, but the restaurant could survive. She put down the phone, feeling slightly better knowing that once she was no longer attached to the restaurant, Toni and his family would be okay.

But would she be okay?

Chapter 20

"Dani?" Toni jerked awake, his head pounding and his gaze blurry. It took him a moment to realize he was on a couch. He scanned the room.

An open bottle of wine and two dirty glasses sat on the coffee table, his suit jacket was draped over a nearby chair, and his phone vibrated then fell onto the floor.

Unable to reach it, he groaned and let his head fall back to the pillow. He'd accidently fallen asleep at Ava's. He jerked back up and checked that he was still wearing pants. He was. Then he rubbed his eyes, trying to remember the events of the night before.

Sophia was abnormally upset but she wouldn't talk about it. And he'd gotten tired. His body had ached with tension and what was supposed to be a quick rest before driving back became a night on the couch.

He still hadn't spoken to Dani. He still didn't know what to say. He rolled half off the couch and grabbed his phone from the floor. His mother had called three times. Then left a text saying Dani had left and he needed to call her.

The second text was from Dani with nothing but the link to a review. He opened the review and groaned again. They would recover, he told himself. Marcello would get better and they could turn it around. But what did that mean for Dani?

He dialed her number, then cut off the call when Ava shuffled by in a long T-shirt.

"*Buongiorno*, Antonio." She gathered the wine bottle and empty glasses, bending over to reveal the tops of her thighs. She wasn't wearing panties.

Toni practically jumped from the couch and strode into the bathroom. Minutes later he emerged less rumpled and Ava was in the kitchen making breakfast.

"Thanks for letting me stay last night. I'm heading back. Tell Sophia I'll call her later."

"No breakfast?"

"No, thank you." He strode down the hall as she called after him.

"Good luck. I'm sorry it didn't go well last night. It was inevitable, really. I mean the kitchen looked a mess when I saw it. Honestly, where did you find her?"

Toni let his hand drop from the doorknob and he walked back into the kitchen.

"What do you mean when you saw it?"

"You know. I just peeked my head in and they were all just standing around."

"Why would you go into the kitchen?"

"Well…" Ava fiddled with her hair. "I was—"

Toni strode toward her slowly, alarm bells ringing in his head. "What did you do?"

"Nothing!"

"Ava, did you do something to the food to get back at me?"

"Toni, I would never. I just… I don't trust that chef. And I was right!"

"Ava, you are messing with the livelihood of us all!"

"I didn't do anything!"

"Ava!"

"It was me." The small voice was like a bullet breaking through glass. Toni and Ava stopped and stared at the young lady in her pajamas.

"What did you say?" Toni whispered.

"I put pepper in the food. It was my fault."

Toni couldn't find words. Sophia's face scrunched as tears fell to the floor. Toni ran to her and knelt by her side.

"*Cara mia*, why would you do that?"

"I thought we would have to open again and Dani would have to stay a little longer. And I know—" Her voice got caught and little huffs came out as she cried harder. "I know you like her, Papá."

Was he hearing this right? His baby sabotaged the restaurant so he and Dani could be together a little longer. His heart filled with joy and pride for his loving daughter. And for the knowledge that Dani wasn't to blame. He needed to tell her.

"I'm sorry, Papá."

"I know. We can fix it." He kissed her on the head. "We'll fix it." Toni looked at Ava, her arms crossed as she leaned against the counter. He assumed she was taking issue with the "I know you like her" comment. And he was tired of hiding it. He turned back to Sophia.

"When you see Dani, you have to apologize. Her reputation was hurt too." Sophia's eyes widened.

"She's gonna hate me."

Toni shook his head. "She won't. I'll make sure of it. I have to go."

Toni reached his car door when his phone vibrated again with his mother's call. He answered the phone intent on giving her an update, but she was in tears.

"Go to the hospital," she commanded. "Now."

"Pneumonia, the doctor said, which is why they were waiting to operate. He wasn't responding to the treatment. And now..." Grace burst into tears and Toni hugged her closer to his side. Ava held Sophia as the four of them stood in the empty room staring at Marcello's empty bed. He went peacefully that morning the doctor assured them.

Toni felt numb. Yesterday morning they had everything and in twenty-four hours his life had changed forever. His uncle was gone, the restaurant was a disaster and he was scared to death that he was losing Dani, as well. He had called her, but she didn't answer. And death wasn't the type of thing you left in a voice mail.

What was he going to do. What the hell was he going to do?

A soft gasp behind him broke his thoughts. Dani's hand was at her mouth, her eyes wide as she fixated on the empty bed. Her head began a slow shake. "No. Please no."

Toni rushed to her and she was in his arms. She clung on to him hard, her body shaking with uncontrollable tears. "How?" she choked out as she pulled back.

"Pneumonia. I called to tell you but you didn't answer."

"I was probably on the train. They called me because they had me down as family from the first night."

"You are family," Toni whispered. "We have to talk."

Dani's gaze shifted to Ava, then back to him. She wriggled from his arms. Her voice sounded cold. "Yes, we do."

They walked down the hall out of earshot. Toni moved closer, letting his hands run over her shoulders, but she stopped him, stepping out of his reach.

He frowned but let her move from him regardless of how awful it felt.

"Did you get my text?"

"I did. I read the review—"

"I think as long as you make a big splash about replacing me, you'll be fine. I don't know what happened, Toni, but as chef I was responsible. There isn't much more I can say—"

"It was Sophia."

"What was Sophia?"

"Sophia spiked the food. She thought you would stay longer if the restaurant didn't open."

Dani blinked with realization, and then her shoulders

slumped with relief. "I've been racking my brain, Toni. It feels good just to know what happened."

"I know what you mean."

Dani's face lit up, then it fell. "I almost said Marcello will understand." Her lip trembled. He wanted to kiss her tears away, but she had a determined look on her face to say more.

"I'm going home in two days. I have an editorial with my mother tomorrow. Then we are heading home."

"Back to New York?"

"I was thinking of trying California. LA needs chefs too."

"What if *I* need you?"

"You don't need me. You need a chef with a reputation for excellence. Not a ghost chef with a trail of disasters behind her."

"That's not what I'm talking about and you know it."

"I thought you slept with Ava last night." She put her hand up at his instant protests. "I know you didn't but I also know you aren't looking to get seriously involved and honestly neither am I. I don't know where I'm going to end up. I have to focus on me first and a temporary fling won't let me do that."

Toni held his tongue. He watched her face as she spoke. He wanted to touch the soft skin of her cheek and kiss her full lips. Even as she told him she was leaving. She was always leaving, he knew that and once again he let his heart run him into a wall.

Because of Ava, he had taken a break from dating, but that was before he realized he couldn't keep his hands from Dani. She had everything he wanted in a woman, save one. Stability. It was important to him, and her plans didn't feel stable at all.

"So you no longer want us to see each other."

"It sounds so formal when you say it like that. I'm saying my leaving might be for the best."

They blinked at each other for a moment, but Toni didn't get a chance to respond. Sophia tapped Dani on the shoulder and confessed. His little girl was so brave, he thought as Dani hugged her and told her everything was fine.

They watched Sophia run back into the room, then turned to each other, unable to ignore the pull between them any longer. Dani cried as their mouths fused in one long last kiss. They clutched each other hard, wishes on their lips and promises in the strokes of their tongues.

Dani pulled back first and looked at him long and hard. "Goodbye, Toni." And on that whisper, she was gone.

"What do you mean she's gone? Gone where?"

Grace glared at him the next day when Toni headed back to his mother's for a lunch. His mother was distraught for many reasons and he gritted his teeth against the anger she was directing toward him. Not that it wasn't warranted. He'd been struggling with the thought of her leaving. Her words made him feel like he'd lost his heart, leaving only a functional shell.

"Back to the States. She leaves tomorrow I think."

"Then she's still here. Go get her." His mother paced, her eyes flashing. "Why would you let her go?"

He was asking himself that too.

"She doesn't want to stay, Ma!"

"Did you tell her you love her?"

"Oh my God…" Toni looked at his mother like she was crazy, but her eyes only held anguish. He lowered his voice and hung his head. "No."

Grace cursed under her breath.

"I'm not sure she feels the same."

"How will you know unless you put it out there?" She

hugged him and kissed him on both cheeks. A knock on the front door sent Grace into the other room, while Toni stared out the window at the restaurant. All night he wished he could have redone their talk in the hospital. Over and over he asked himself if he had told her he loved her, would she have agreed to stay?

Antonio turned as footsteps came toward the kitchen and Grace entered, followed by an older gentleman in a suit. Grace introduced them.

"Antonio, this is Signore Russo, Marcello's lawyer. It seems he changed his will days before he passed away." The men shook hands and the three of them took a seat at the table. The lawyer was slow in his delivery, pulling out stacks of papers with Marcello's signature, explaining the reason he had come to his mother's home.

"It's fortunate I have you both here," he started, fumbling for his glasses. Toni's mother looked at him from out of the side of her eye when he started reading a bunch of legal mumbo jumbo, which he said in a monotone that had Toni almost asleep. "To my loving sister and executor of my estate, I leave my home and possessions to do with as you please and one-third of my restaurant Via Carciofo. To my loving nephew I leave my wine cellar and one-third of my restaurant Via Carciofo."

Toni and his mother gave each other a look as Signore Russo passed around papers to be signed. After gathering the documents, he put them back in his briefcase and shut the top.

"Grazie," Signore Russo said as he stood and turned to leave.

"Wait," Toni said after he jumped from his seat. "Who has the last third?"

The old man fixed his glasses on his nose. "I am unable to give you that information."

Grace came forward. "But they will be our partner. How can you not tell us?"

"I must find them and tell them first. If I can find them." The latter he said under his breath as he labored toward the front door. Toni was following him close behind and stopped him one last time at the door.

"Signore, I may be able to help you find this man. Then you could go home and relax, huh?"

Russo narrowed his gaze and looked around to see who was listening. Then he leaned toward Toni. "It's a woman."

A thankful smile spread wide across Toni's face. "I know where she is."

Chapter 21

"Look at this skin, it's perfect." Dani closed her eyes as Roberto pressed a spongy thing all over her face. If her skin was so perfect, why did she need so much foundation?

"Those are my genes, Roberto, make no mistake." Her mother was next to her, putting on her own false eyelashes in the mirror while three stylists buzzed behind them putting together the looks for the shoot.

"I know it. She's like your Mini-Me. Okay, Mini-Me, look up." Dani gritted her teeth as a mascara brush was dangerously close to her eyeball.

Walking through the offices of *Vogue* had been a bit of a dream come true, but sitting in a chair for hours in a small dingy dressing room? Not so much.

Roberto hummed RuPaul as he worked, instructing her to look up, then down, then purse her lips, then make an O. "This is so exciting. Mommy dearest is going to show you the ropes!"

Francesca's interrupted her blowout to turn her head. "Stop calling me that. I am not Joan Crawford." Her mother turned toward the mirror with a sultry look. "More like Dorothy Dandridge."

"Well, I heard she was crazy too," Roberto snickered. "Okay, all done. Open those eyes, Mini-Me."

Dani blinked at her reflection. She wasn't even sure it was her. If she saw a picture of this woman she'd think she was…gorgeous. Her gaze shifted to Roberto.

"You're a genius."

Roberto nodded. "I am. But you didn't need much help, Mini-Me. A little mascara here, some eyeliner there, and a BB cream to even out your skin tone. You're hot. Oh, to be young again. Right, Fannie?"

"You said it, Robbie." Francesca looked at her. "You look stunning, sweetheart."

Stunning. The word brought back heart-wrenching memories. She hadn't heard from him, which she supposed was normal when you said goodbye to someone, but in this case she was hoping he wouldn't listen.

She'd had fantasies of him barging into the hotel and declaring his love. Or at least a declarative phone call. She'd even accept a text.

"What's wrong, Danica?" Roberto put his hands on her shoulders and peered at her reflection.

"Nothing. I'm fine. Just nervous."

"She's having man trouble," her mother said, shaking out her roller-curled hair.

"Humph, aren't we all?" Roberto pursed his lips. "What'd he do? Cheat? Take your money? Is it drugs?"

"Robbie, who are you dating? Convicts?" said her mother.

He shrugged. "You know who I'm talking about."

"Oh jeez." Her mother rolled her eyes and Dani smiled at their easy friendship. Roberto turned to Dani and put a finger over his lips as he whispered.

"He's famous." Roberto giggled. "Dani, tell me everything."

"There isn't much to tell. He lives here and I don't. Plus he has family drama to work out. It's best that we ended our relationship."

Roberto stared at her with a sad face. "That sounds very mature. But why can't you find a job here and stay?"

"She doesn't want to. She wants to come to California with me," her mother said.

Roberto looked at her from the side of his eye. "You're

here all the time. You can visit her." He turned to Dani. "Are you in love with him?"

Dani blinked at her reflection, and then her eyes slid toward her mother's watchful gaze. She was relieved when the head stylists announced it was time for wardrobe.

They chose three looks for them both: denim, casual and glam. Dani posed with her mother for the first few shoots, feeling more comfortable by the time they got to the glam shoot.

Her red sleeveless bodycon dress had lace along her midriff and upper chest so only one solid covered her breasts. Paired with black heels, it was the epitome of sexy. And it fit perfectly.

She didn't "suck it in" nor was she instructed to pose a certain way to minimize her body. She had fun with her mother and at the end of her shoot, she felt beautiful. Like a Botticelli.

Would she ever stop thinking of him?

Then her mother posed alone for the cover shoot and things got intense. Dani overheard the photographer whispering about her loose skin, her sagging breasts, her small belly. There was the ugliness her mother had tried to keep from her.

Head high, Francesca walked off the photo shoot amid a round of applause, but when she got to the dressing room, she was depleted.

She magically took her strapless push-up bra off from under her dress and threw it on the counter.

"That was killing me."

"You looked amazing, Mother."

"I hate that photographer." Francesca then turned to Dani. "Are you sure you want to come to LA?"

"Yes," Dani shrugged. "I think I could find work there."

Francesca lowered her gaze, then turned back to her

mirror. "Roberto and I are going for dinner. Would you like to come? Oh, by the way. The dress and shoes you're wearing as well as the others are yours to keep."

"Nice perk."

"That doesn't always happen. But I wanted you to have them."

"Thank you, for the dresses. And for today." She felt closer to her mother in the last twenty-four hours than she ever had, but she still couldn't pull herself out of the dumps. Nor could she get Toni off of her mind. "I'm going to head back to the hotel."

Thirty minutes later Dani walked into her hotel lobby and turned her head at the concierge's soft gasp and nod of approval. Maybe she should have joined her mother and Roberto, she thought. Why let this make up and dress go to waste.

She was almost to the elevators when someone called out her name.

She slowly turned and scanned the lobby just as Toni stood from one of the lounge chairs.

Dani felt her heart flip-flop in her chest. Her first instinct was to run to him and throw her arms around his neck. Instead she gave him a neutral smile and strode toward him, frowning when an older man with a briefcase stood when she arrived.

"Hi, Toni."

"Dani." His gaze was fixed on her face, then traveled up and down her dress. His hands went in his pockets, and then he brought them back out. "Um, this is Signore Russo. He, um, he's handling Marcello's will. Why are you dressed like this?"

"I had a photo shoot with my mother. Did you say Marcello's will?"

"Oh, okay. And yes," he sighed, still staring at her with an intense gaze.

"You seem relieved."

"I am." His jaw clenched.

"What did you think I was doing in this dress?"

"Having dinner with someone other than me." Toni's gaze slid to the signore. "Russo needs to speak with you. Do you mind if I stay?"

"Are you going to frown the whole time?"

"Maybe." He gave her his seat and moved to an adjacent one, his gaze still on her.

"What can I do for you, Signore Russo?"

Toni didn't stop looking at her while the old lawyer found his glasses and shuffled through his papers. Toni looked like a lounging tiger ready to strike, his expression like a mask.

"Here we are. Miss Nilsson, you've been named as a beneficiary of one-third owner of Via Carciofo and one-third owner of Via Olivia. And it says here he has left you his knives. If you just sign here, the transactions will be complete."

It took Dani a moment to fully comprehend what Russo was telling her. It must have been all over her face, because Toni leaned over and grabbed her hand. "He left you his shares of the restaurants, Dani."

She squeezed Toni's hand. "And his knives." She was going to cry.

"*Sì*, signora." Once Dani signed her name, Russo handed her his card and left.

Toni took the empty seat in front of her. "Are you okay?"

"I think so. I just can't believe he's gone."

"I know."

"Did you know about the will?"

"I only found out today. He must have loved you very much."

"How do you feel about me having a part of your restaurants?"

"How do I feel?" The edges of his mouth flickered. "I know I said I didn't want to get involved but I haven't felt whole since you told me you were leaving. I don't want to run these restaurants without you. And I can't deny how strong my feelings are for you any longer."

"You have feelings for me?" She didn't dare believe it.

"Dani, you have no idea how much I want to poke out the eyes of every man that has seen you in this dress. You really have no idea how beautiful you are, do you?"

"Toni—"

"I can't stop thinking about you. Tell me you've been thinking about me too."

"I have. But—"

Toni unfolded from his chair, took Dani's hand and pulled her from her seat right into his arms. His mouth was warm and firm and he held her as if she was essential to his existence. Her hands ran over his arms, feeling the power of his body as he bent her back with the force of his need. It matched her own.

Toni eased her away from him when a group of tourists rapidly pressed the elevator button.

"Let's go to your room. This is too public," Toni whispered.

They didn't speak in the elevator, but Toni's hand secretly trailed up and down her back. When they walked down the hallway to Dani's room, Toni kept that hand solidly in the small of her back. Once inside the room, however, they crossed the suite to her bedroom and that hand spun her around and pressed her up against the inside of the door.

Their mouths fused, fierce and demanding. He pulled back slowly and his fingertips teased over the lace of the dress.

"Do you know how many men were looking at you in the lobby?" he said, shoving out of his jacket. His hand gripped then caressed her throat as he spoke, and then he turned her face to nip and suck at her neck. "Those men wanted to make love to you." He pulled back to look at her, his gaze burning with lust. "Just the thought of them touching you makes me crazy."

"Well, now you know how it feels. How is Ava doing?" His eyes flared.

"Ava is well aware of who I want." He jerked off his jacket and tossed it on the chair. Then she saw his gaze drop to her packed bags in the corner of the room. "How about I help you unpack those bags?"

"Why should I stay?" Dani remained against the wall, watching him prowl the room like a panther. His hands went from his pockets to run through his hair and back. She knew his cues now. Emotions were boiling she just needed them to spill over.

"You have a business to run now."

"Why shouldn't I just sell my shares to you and go home?" He ripped off his tie and threw it on the dresser.

"I'm not buying your shares."

"Someone will buy them." His eyes flashed.

"Don't you dare."

"I dare you to tell me why I should stay?"

He stopped then and stared at her. His mouth opened then closed. "We want to open the restaurant for good next week in Marcello's honor. He would want you to cook."

She slumped away from the wall and stalked toward him. She grabbed the back of his head.

"You chickenshit." Her lips crashed against his and Toni kissed her back with abandon.

He gently peeled her out of the dress, taking extra care with the lace fabric, kissing and sucking the newly exposed skin. Her bra and panties disappeared like smoke. "Leave the shoes," he instructed, ripping off his shirt and undoing his pants. "And get on the bed."

Dani lay back and reached for Toni. He stood over her, shirt gone, pants unbuckled. His gaze racked over her body.

"You're incredible," he murmured, pulling himself out of his pants and stroking the long length.

She was aching for him, getting hotter and wetter watching him run his hands over himself.

"Toni—" she breathed, his possessive attitude making her hotter and hotter.

"Spread your legs for me," he instructed, and her knees fell open at his command. "Mine," he murmured.

Her heart almost jumped out of her chest, desire pulsing through her at the thought of being solely his possession.

He lowered his mouth and nuzzled her breasts, his lips nipping and sucking her nipples until she was writhing uncontrollably.

"Turn over—get on your hands and knees for me." His voice was laced with raw need, making her shudder at the sound. She did as he asked and flipped her hair as she turned back to look at him.

She felt his palm smack then knead one bare cheek. The other hand smoothed over her shoulder and executed a light grip.

"You're not leaving," he breathed into her ear.

Then he thrust into her in one hard surge, burying his impressive length all at once. Dani moaned as the strength of his hips drove her face closer to the bed.

He groaned and stilled, bending to give her a small kiss on her back, and his hands settled on her hips in a strong grip.

He pounded into her, thick and strong, filling her fully with every relentless pump of his hips. One hand grabbed the heel of her black stiletto and bent her knee up, pushing her forward and opening her hips even more.

Dani clawed at the duvet as he drove deeper still, feeling like he was taking over her entire body.

He was wild and unapologetic inside her, and she loved every minute of it. Never had any man made her feel so desired.

She cried out as she came all around him, her swollen flesh gripping him, and pulled a throaty yelp from his throat.

Her body jolted and stars burst behind her eyes, yet he still surged hard and sure, gripped her body even more.

"You can't imagine how it feels," he said, his voice low in her ear as he leaned over her, "to have you come while I'm inside you."

Toni exploded in a rush of grunts as he thrust himself into her one final time, his hands digging into her skin as he rode out his orgasm deep within her.

They fell onto the bed into a heap of sweaty skin and heavy breathing, rolling over to lay next to each other. Toni moved onto his elbow and traced one of Dani's nipples with his fingertip. Dani let her eyes drift shut.

"I have to leave town for a couple days," he said, his voice throaty and full. "But I'll be back in time for the opening." His hand caressed her cheek, then gently turned her face toward his. "Unpack those bags. You're not leaving."

Dani opened her eyes and studied his handsome face. His voice sounded confident, but his eyes held a plea. "I'm staying," she said, looking into his eyes. Then added, "For now."

His brows slashed over his eyes at that comment, but he

stayed quiet. His eyes held a warning that made her smile a little. She wasn't going anywhere, but he didn't need to know that.

She part owned not one but two restaurants, she wasn't going to throw that away.

Dani put on a robe while Toni dressed leisurely, kissing and touching her without hesitation or persuasion, like she was his possession. His woman.

"I'll call you tomorrow from the airport to make sure you haven't changed your mind."

"Yes, sir."

"I like that."

"Don't get used to it."

She walked him to the door and she gave him a long thorough kiss in the threshold.

"Tell Sophia I said hi."

"Yes, Chef."

"I like that."

"Get used to it." He gave her one last quick kiss and turned into the hallway, running straight into Francesca and Roberto. Her mother's eyes were wide and Roberto's hand flew to his chest. Dani could only imagine what she looked like and clutched her robe closed further.

Toni kissed Francesca's hand and nodded a hello to Roberto, and then the three of them watched him walk down the hall. Dani broke the ice.

"So, it looks like I might be staying, after all."

Chapter 22

Three days later Dani donned her black coat and took her place at the kitchen. Her kitchen. It was surreal and she planned on thanking Marcello by cooking the best meal Milan had ever seen.

But by the looks of the dining area, Milan wasn't ready to eat it. It was prime dining hour and several tables were empty.

"Coming in!" She recognized his voice before he entered. Charcoal suit and black tie, Toni looked dashing, and she immediately asked for his touch. It has been too long since the hotel room, but they had spoken every day and sometimes night on the phone. Something had shifted between them. He was more territorial with her well-being, more attentive than before. She had to admit that she liked it.

He greeted the staff, then sent her a wicked smile. She noticed a medium-size shopping bag in his hand. "Chef, may I see you in my office?" That meant the meat locker. She entered the cold storage room and was immediately pulled into a feverish kiss. Three days of pent-up desire rushed through them both. "Miss me?"

"Of course. How was business?"

His gaze roamed over her face. "I got what I needed." In their phone conversations he'd been cagey about what he was doing. Something about the warehouses blah, blah, blah. She got the sense it was something else too. He had hinted as much.

"And what was that?"

He presented the bag and she reached inside, delighted

to find a familiar rolled knife bag. Marcello's knives. "I had them sharpened."

Tears rose. "That's so thoughtful."

"There's something else in there."

She checked the bag and found a small velvet ring box. Her heart thumped as she met his steady gaze. He nodded. "Open it."

There were no words. A canary yellow diamond as big as her knuckle sat in a platinum setting of diamond baguettes.

"I love you, Danica Nilsson. And I want to spend the rest of my life with you. I would have told you the other night, but it didn't feel right without the ring. Regardless of what happens with the restaurants, I want you to know that I need you in my life."

She could no longer hold back the tears. She stared at the ring, her mind racing and her heart full for the man that stood in front of her. In her meat locker. She laughed.

"You're laughing."

"I'm not! This is just surreal."

"Say yes."

"Toni—"

"Look who's chickenshit now."

"Yes! You bully. Yes! I love you and I want to marry you."

Their kiss was freezing cold and wonderful. He took the ring and brought her hand up to receive it, but she pulled it back. "Toni, I can't cook with that on my finger. I love it, but I can't wear it right now."

He smiled and cocked his head. "I know, Chef, so I got you another one." He pulled another box from his pocket and opened it to reveal an angel hair–thin platinum band encrusted with the smallest diamonds she'd ever seen. It was perfect.

Opening night went without a hitch with Dani working endlessly to prepare her best meal. *Every night is opening night*, as Marcello used to say. She and the staff had begun cleaning when Toni and a wide-eyed server burst into the kitchen holding a table napkin.

"Dani, look at this." She took the outstretched napkin and saw handwriting in pen all over the surface.

"Who defaces a cloth napkin like this?" Dani squinted at the cursive letters.

Toni's eyes flashed. "Read it."

Miss Nilsson, I was devastated to hear of Marcello's passing and had come to this establishment to pay my respects. I know it was supposed to be his triumph. I must tell you that you have big shoes to fill, and from what I can tell, you are wearing them quite comfortably. Velvet artichoke soup? Never have I tasted anything so simple yet so rich. I must confess I was unaware of your contribution to the kitchen of L'Italy in New York until recently. Are you aware they have lost two stars? I will be retracting the scathing review I left. Although if you recall, I said the veal shank was excellent. My review will be posted tomorrow. Good luck, Chef Nilsson. I look forward to more from you.
—The Taste.

One year later

"It's time, Dani." Liz burst through the door of the kitchen, almost knocking over Dao and the tray of chocolates he was preparing. Dani frowned at her friend, who backed away with her hands up.

"Dao, put one of those little chocolates on each of the plates and a drizzle of Lambrusco sauce, please."

"I can't believe you. You have guests out there." Liz put her hands on her hips and raised her brows.

"Almost done." Dani swirled the icing over the seventh tier of the cake. "Dao, it's ready." She handed her sous-chef the knife and watched as her staff carried the cake away. Once she was satisfied that everything was set, she hurried toward the double doors.

"Woman, take that black coat off!"

"Oh!" Dani unbuttoned her chef's coat, revealing a floor-length strapless wedding dress with a mermaid hem and short train. She kicked off her Crocs and slipped her feet into her sparkly Jimmy Choos.

Liz tsked, then smiled at her friend. "You look gorgeous."

Dani walked with Liz back into the dining room, her eyes settling happily on their hundreds of guests, most of whom she had just met. But her heart filled to see Destin and Nicole, her mother, Grace and Sophia, and her father chatting animatedly with Toni.

She strode toward the two, her father looking stately in his suit, his neck tattoos peeking from the collar also making him look like an older David Beckham. "You look lovely, darling." Her father wound an arm around her shoulders and kissed her hair.

"Thank you, Daddy. You look nice too."

"Do you think your mother thinks so?"

Francesca was watching them from the side of her eye, and then she quickly turned away. She was ravishing in a blue sequined gown, and she knew it. Francesca was doing her best impression of ignoring her father, but it seemed a little more like foreplay. Gross. "Yeah, I think she does." Dani turned to her husband. "We have a cake to cut."

"Yes, Chef."

Dani spread Marcello's knives on the table and cut her husband a generous slice of marble cake with lots of red wine buttercream icing. His finger made it into the slice before she could serve him.

"You are asking for it."

"And I hope I get it," he said after sucking his finger. "Will you make this for me every night?"

She held his piece to his mouth and their eyes met in challenge. If she smashed the cake on him, he'd do it to her. She let him have his cake and when it came her turn, he was behaved, if not a little impish when he slid a fingertip into the icing and slipped a little more between her lips. He didn't know it yet, but she had made extra icing.

The crowd cheered and her staff rushed in to cut and serve.

"Where is the champagne?"

"I vetoed the champagne."

Her husband's head whipped around. "What? Why? I had the warehouse send the Clos." He looked over her head and whatever he was going to say died on his lips. The staff was pouring sparkling red for their guests.

"It's the Dolcetto. Marcello's Dolcetto. I asked them to bring it from our warehouse, but don't worry, as your supplier I made sure you got a discount."

His eyes were filled with love. "That's cute. Come here."

They kissed among yells and clinking glasses.

"Are you ready for your cake? It's the chef's special," Dani whispered, suggestively rubbing against him.

"You get the icing," Toni teased.

"And you get the Clos."

Toni's smile was wicked. "*Sì*, Chef. Whatever you want, Chef. Forever."

* * * * *

COMING NEXT MONTH
Available July 17, 2018

#581 ONE PERFECT MOMENT
The Taylors of Temptation • **by A.C. Arthur**
TV producer Ava Cannon is stunned to discover that the lover who briefly shared her bed is one of America's most famous sextuplets. But Dr. Gage Taylor now shuns the spotlight. As they rekindle their affair, will Ava have to choose between a game-changing career move and her love?

#582 CAMPAIGN FOR HIS HEART
The Cardinal House • **by Joy Avery**
Former foster child Lauder Tolson is running for North Carolina state senate, but he needs a girlfriend for the campaign. The ideal candidate is childhood nemesis Willow Dawson. To fulfill her own dream, she agrees. Soon, they're a devoted couple in public, but neither expects how hot it gets in private.

#583 PATH TO PASSION
The Astacios • **by Nana Prah**
Heir to his family's global empire, branding genius Miguel Astacio turns everything into marketing gold. Only his best friend's sister seems immune to his magic touch. Until Tanya Carrington comes to him to save her floundering nightclub. Miguel is ready to rectify past mistakes. But will he win her heart?

#584 UNCONDITIONALLY MINE
Miami Dreams • **by Nadine Gonzalez**
Event planner Sofia Silva is keeping a secret. No one can know that her engagement to her cheating fiancé is over. Until she meets gorgeous, wealthy newcomer Jonathan Gunther. When he invites Sofia to lie low at his house, their attraction explodes…but will her dilemma ruin their chance at forever?

KPCNM0718

Get 2 Free Books,
Plus 2 Free Gifts—
just for trying the Reader Service!

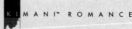

Want to give in to temptation with
steamy tales of irresistible desire?

Check out **Harlequin® Presents®**,
Harlequin® Desire and
Harlequin® Kimani™ Romance books!

New books available every month!

CONNECT WITH US AT:

Harlequin.com/Community

 Facebook.com/HarlequinBooks

 Twitter.com/HarlequinBooks

 Instagram.com/HarlequinBooks

 Pinterest.com/HarlequinBooks

ReaderService.com

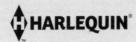

**ROMANCE WHEN
YOU NEED IT**

PGENRE2017